Divine
INTERVENTION

By P.L. Byers

Divine INTERVENTION

P.L. Byers

DELLARTE
PRESS

Dellarte Press books may be ordered through booksellers or by contacting:

Dellarte Press™
1663 Liberty Drive
Bloomington, IN 47403
www.dellartepress.com
1-877-217-3420

ISBN: 978-1-4501-0023-6 (sc)
ISBN: 978-1-4501-0025-0 (hc)
ISBN: 978-1-4501-0024-3 (e)

Printed in the United States of America

Dellarte Press rev. date: 2/18/2013

Dedication

To my wonderful husband Mark for encouraging me to follow my dream. To two amazing young men (Justin and Charlie) who mean the world to me and to my parents who always made me feel like I could do anything I wanted.....thank you!!

Lastly and more importantly to my sister Lisa, thanks for your inputs and patience with my nagging to "read" this. Your insights and suggestions make me better! I love you all!!

Chapter 1

THE WEATHER OUTSIDE REFLECTED SABRINA WALLACE'S mood. As the rain beat against her bedroom window, she continued to pack the few suitcases she would need for her trip. While flying was not one of her favorite things to do, it was important for her job. Sort of like eating spinach or liver; not exactly something she liked, but it was good for her so she did it. Flying was a necessary evil in her business. As one of the brightest up and coming architects, her clients were not always just a short drive away. Her growing reputation was a great source of pride for her, but it also required her to travel farther afield to meet with clients. While her residence and offices were located in Boston Massachusetts, she was becoming well known enough to have clients all over the United States. So over the years, she learned to set aside her fear of flying. Her personal assistant and best friend Katherine Manning, always teased her about her fear. It amused her that such a put together woman in the board room could have such a fear of flying.

Sabrina remembered how she and Katherine met. It was right after her parents were killed in an automobile accident seven years earlier. Katherine had been Sabrina's father's assistant for several years. After their death, Sabrina couldn't bring herself to go to her father's office to pack his personal items so Katherine did it for her. When she brought them to Sabrina, Katherine found a pale and lethargic young woman who simply sat around her apartment, giving in to her grief. Katherine immediately took Sabrina under her wing, forcing her to join the land of the living. Although they were very close in age, Katherine was able to give Sabrina the strength and support she needed. Gently guiding Sabrina through the months of grief, anger, and shock, it only seemed natural for Katherine to become Sabrina's assistant when she began her own architectural firm.

The telephone rang startling Sabrina from her thoughts. "Hello?"

"Hi champ. Ready for your flight?"

Sabrina smiled into the receiver. "As ready as I'll ever be. Anything new to report before I head out?"

"Nope. Everything is still set like we discussed earlier. Just wanted to make sure you didn't need anything. I'm headed out for my hot date."

"Who is it this time?"

"I'll fill you in if it works out. Are you sure you don't want me to give you a lift to the airport?"

"Thanks, Kat, but I'm happy taking a cab. Is the car rental all set when I land in San Francisco?"

"It's all with your airline ticket. If you have any problems just call me on the cell phone. Have a safe trip. See you in a few days."

"Bye. Thanks for everything. Good luck on your hot date. I hope this one has teeth," Sabrina joked, remembering Katherine's description of her last blind date that featured a bad toupee and three missing front teeth.

"Me too. See ya!"

After circling the apartment to make sure that she didn't forget anything, Sabrina went downstairs to the lobby to hail a cab. Thankfully, living in Boston made it easy to get a cab. Not that the cab rides were any less terrifying than a flight, but at least it made getting to Logan Airport a little easier.

Once Sabrina was checked in, she made her way to the departure gate to await the boarding call. After only a few minutes, her flight was called, and with an uneasy feeling, she boarded her flight.

~

ALEXANDER DELUCA LOOKED AT HIS WATCH for the third time in only a few minutes. If his calculations were correct, he would have just enough time to make it to Logan Airport. If he didn't, it wouldn't be the first flight he missed. As the CEO of Deluca Enterprises, an investment firm he and his brother started ten years earlier, Alex missed many flights due to last-minute problems that had to be ironed out.

There were times when he wished his younger brother, Sam, would take more of an interest in the company he had agreed to be a part of. Alex's intention of starting the company with his brother was to have something they could share together. Sam and Alex grew up in a loving household with all the advantages most kids only dreamed of having. For Alex, it only made him work harder so that society wouldn't think he got where he was because it was handed to him. Sam on the other hand didn't care what people thought and went about the business of his life without a care in the world, knowing that Deluca Enterprises was in the capable hands of his brother. Sam was the handsome, easy-going brother who basked in their parent's love. Alex doubted if there was anything Sam could do that would upset their parents. Alex, on the other hand, was the dark, mysterious brother his parents couldn't seem to figure out. They loved him unconditionally, though, and Alex knew it.

After packing a few more things into his briefcase, Alex grabbed his suit jacket and started for the door. Before he reached it however, Mary Simms, his assistant, buzzed him.

"Excuse me, Mr. Deluca?"

Impatiently Alex walked over to his desk and pushed the intercom button. "Yes Mary, what is it? I'm on my way out."

"I'm sorry, Mr. Deluca, but your brother is on the phone and said it was important."

Alex smiled ruefully and shook his head. "Thanks, Mary. I'll take it." Alex pushed the flashing button on the phone. "What now, Sam? Did you lose your credit card again?"

"Very funny, Alex. I only did that once, and you'll never let me forget it, will you?"

"Sorry. I'm on my way to the airport. What's up?"

"Leaving town again?"

"I wouldn't have to if you would be more than a silent partner in this company. I could use the help, you know."

"Now, Alex, we've been through this a million times."

"I know, I know. You're still sowing your wild oats. To what do I owe the pleasure of this phone call?"

"I wanted to see if you'd like to join me in New Hampshire this weekend for a little fun."

"I know it's not skiing, since it's the middle of August, so what's up?"

"Two beautiful girls!"

"No thanks, Sam. I have neither the time nor the interest. Besides, I'm on my way out west to iron out a new contract."

"You know that Mom is really beginning to worry about you. All work, no play. You're honestly becoming a dull boy, Alex."

"No, I'm becoming a rich man."

"You're already a rich man. There's more to life, you know. You're going to give yourself ulcers before you realize it. Ever since that Jessica girl left you, you're more of a recluse than ever."

Alex briefly thought of the tall, leggy brunette who broke his heart. Just when he thought he had found the woman he could possibly share his life with, she up and left him. Accusations of being emotionally detached and only caring about his job flitted through his mind.

"Look, Sam, I appreciate the offer, but I have to catch a flight. I'll call you when I get back. We'll do something then, okay?"

"Fine. Have a safe flight. Bye."

"Bye, Sam." Alex hung the telephone up and once again walked to the door. On the way out, he briefly stopped to talk to Mary about a few things she needed to care of while he was gone and then went out to hail a cab.

Twenty minutes later, Alexander Deluca was racing through the airport to make his flight on Pentium Airways. Still cursing the fact that he was flying coach as opposed to his usual first-class arrangements, he made it to the gate just in time. Booking at the last minute, he knew he was lucky just to have a seat on the flight at all! With only a few minutes to spare and an odd feeling in his stomach, he boarded the plane for the long flight to California.

Chapter 2

SABRINA LOOKED AROUND THE AIRPLANE AT the other passengers. Observing the different people always helped to keep her mind off the fact that she was stranded inside a large metal object racing at high speeds through the clouds, relying on a few engines to keep her in the air.

In the seat in front of her, was a rather harried looking young mother with a baby girl. The little girl was intent on standing on her mother's lap, facing the back of the plane to see better what was going on behind her. To Sabrina, the little girl looked to be about seven months old. She had a sweet, round face with chestnut-colored hair and hazel eyes. The single tooth in the center of her wide grin was a comical vision to behold. This was definitely a little girl who could have any adult wrapped around her chubby little fingers. The proof was in the way the passengers near the girl were trying valiantly to coax a grin from her.

Across the aisle was a teenager with headphones sprouting from his ears. Even from across that distance, Sabrina could hear the faint sound of some heavy-metal band. It would be a miracle, Sabrina thought, if the young man would still have his hearing in another ten years. Of course, she never listened to music that loud when she was a teen.

Next to the teenager, in the window seat, sat a very attractive man wearing a rather serious-looking power suit and tie. He had an air about him that didn't encourage friendly conversation. It was a good thing they weren't sitting close enough for a conversation, Sabrina thought. She would have been tempted to try to irritate him with idle chatter just because she was bored.

Sabrina was seated in the isle and next to her by the window was a pleasant older gentleman who was on his way to visit his daughter and grandson in California. He was an easy going man and pleasant to talk with. He showed Sabrina pictures of his family. It was obvious by the smiling faces of the people in the photos that they were a happy family, making Sabrina long for one that she lost. She tried very hard not to feel sorry for herself for not having her family with her but there were times, like this, when it bothered her.

After an hour or so into the flight, the stewardesses served drinks, snacks and to those willing to cough up a small fortune, a dried sandwich or a simple lunch. Sabrina ate a few bites, worked on some paperwork for a while before becoming drowsy. She fought it for a while, then gave up and settled in for a little nap.

Sabrina wasn't sure what woke her, but she had a very strange feeling when she opened her eyes. Becoming more alert, she looked around and saw concern on the faces around her. She sat up straighter and asked the gentleman next to her what was wrong.

"Don't know Miss. The plane just made an awful noise and started pitching a few minutes ago."

Just then the pilot came on the intercom. "Ladies and gentlemen, we are experiencing a few mechanical difficulties. We're going to start a decent to land at the Lincoln Municipal Airport in Nebraska. We ask that, as a precaution, you make sure that your seat belts are securely fastened. Flight attendants, please be seated."

Sabrina looked around and saw the look of panic on the other passengers faces. Quickly she said a silent prayer and checked her seat belt to make sure that it was fastened. When she looked to her left, her gaze was met by the handsome gentleman in the power suit. When she turned to look forward again, she saw a wave of smoke coming toward her......

~

ALEX FELT THE JOLT OF THE airplane and knew that something serious was going on. He'd been on many flights and had never experienced anything like what was happening. As the plane continued its descent he checked his seatbelt. He glanced to his right and his eyes met those of the woman he noticed earlier. He saw the look of terror on her face and tried to send her a silent message to have faith, that things would be okay. When he saw her look ahead, his eyes followed the same direction and he too saw the smoke filling the cabin. Suddenly the passengers began screaming and the airplane took a sudden pitch forward and careened nose first towards the ground......

Chapter 3

SABRINA GRADUALLY BECAME AWARE OF HOW cold she was. Thinking she was still on the plane, she tried to sit up but found that she couldn't move. She blinked her eyes a few times and shook her head. It was then that she smelled fuel and smoke. As she focused her eyes, Sabrina realized she was no longer on the plane, but on the ground with parts of the airplane littered around her. Gradually she started moving her head to look around. Shock set in as she began to realize that bodies and parts of the plane were scattered around her. Hearing a loud, agonizing scream, she was surprised to realize it was her own voice, and not that of someone else.

Okay Sabrina, she lectured herself. Get a hold of yourself. You're still alive. She began calling to see if there were any other survivors but no one answered her pleas. When she tried to move, Sabrina realized she was pinned beneath wreckage from the plane and she couldn't feel her legs. Slowly she began to examine her other body parts to see if everything else was intact. Other than cuts and bruises, her ribs seemed to bring her the most pain. When she started to lay her head back down, she heard a small whimper coming from her right side. When she turned her head, she caught sight of a little tuft of hair. Realizing that it was the baby that had been sitting in front of her, she tried to reach for her. After a few seconds of trying to wiggle over, Sabrina was able to grab a hold of the little girl's hand. Fortunately, the baby was not pinned under anything so Sabrina gently pulled the little girl toward her, until she rested against her side.

"Okay little one," Sabrina crooned. "Looks like it's you and me for a while. Don't worry; I'll try to keep you warm. I'm sure that people are on their way to rescue us."

Sabrina kept talking to the little girl in a soft voice to try and soothe her as she checked her over for injuries as best as she could from her pinned angle. There was nothing obvious except for some cuts. The little girl was so calm though, Sabrina was more nervous than ever. She should be screaming, she thought, not just lying so still and quiet.

Sabrina wrapped her arms around the little girl and pulled her closer. Please God, she prayed. Get us help fast. And with that silent prayer hanging in the air, Sabrina slipped unconscious once again.

~

AS ALEX CAME TO, HE REALIZED that the plane had definitely crashed. The deafening silence was what hit him the hardest. If there were other survivors, there would be screams or pleas for help. But there were none. Not even the sound of sirens and people coming to rescue them. Just the quietness of the wind and the crackling of small fires left burning around him. When he looked around, he saw sights so horrifying; he knew he would live with the images for the rest of his life. He also noticed how dense the area was where they were. No wonder he thought, that help had not come yet. There was no easy access to get to where the plane had crashed. It could take hours, much less days to get to them.

Alex began checking to see what injuries he had. He was pinned under part of a wing, but he could at least feel his toes and wiggle them. His left arm was definitely broken, not to mention a few ribs. When he reached up to touch his head, he felt a large bump and warm sticky blood oozing from the wound. His vision was blurred a little so Alex simply closed his eyes and laid his head back down. After he rested for a few minutes, he lifted his head again to look around. When he yelled for help, in case anyone was near, he noticed a slim hand near him. He reached over to see if he could feel a pulse and realized that the hand was warm to the touch. He gently shook the hand and was relieved to hear a soft moan.

"Lady, wake up. Can you hear me?" he desperately pleaded.

When a few seconds went by with no response, Alex tried again.

"Lady, wake up. Can you hear me?"

Sabrina slowly came awake and looked to where the voice was coming from. "So we're not the only ones."

"No, but I can't hear or see anyone else. Is there someone else near you?"

"Yes, the little girl that was sitting in the seat in front of me. She's here beside me. I'm trying to keep her warm. I can't see any injuries on her but she's very quiet." Sabrina touched the little girls face and realized that she was very cold. Sometime after she went unconscious, the little girl must have passed quietly away.

"Noooo," Sabrina screamed. "Please God no! She was so little and so innocent." Sabrina gently held the lifeless body of the little girl against her side and softly touched her face and head as she sobbed for the loss of such a sweet child.

Hearing the anguished cries, Alex reached for the hand of the woman whose heartache was so palatable it broke his heart, and held tightly to her.

"Listen to me. You did everything you could. She was hurt too badly to survive. There was nothing you could have done to help her."

"But she was so young and innocent" Sabrina sobbed.

Not knowing what else to do, Alex simply held on to Sabrina's hand while she cried. As time creped slowly by, that's how the two remained. Hands entangled, trying desperately to give strength to each other, hoping that rescue would come quickly. The human contact served to remind both of them that even though death and destruction was all around them, they were indeed still alive.

Eventually to pass the time and to keep each other from thinking about what lay around them, Alex and Sabrina began talking. After exchanging names, they talked about themselves, what they did for a living and why they were on the flight to begin with. Alex talked about his family and how worried they must be and Sabrina told him about her family and how she had lost her parents a few years before. As the hours wore on, a bond formed between them. They kept each other busy talking so neither of them would have time to think about their situation and where they were or the fact that it was getting dark. When they eventually heard the sounds of rescuers plowing their way to them, it was a strange mix of emotions. Sad for what lay around them, then triumphant. They had both survived!

Chapter 4

IT TOOK SOME TIME FOR THE rescuers to get to the location of where the plane had gone down. Debris littered the ground making it difficult to maneuver. The dense forest didn't help either. Between cutting through trees and underbrush, it was tedious job but the volunteers worked tirelessly, trying to get to anybody who may have survived.

When the call had come in that a plane had gone down in the area, there was an uneasy feeling among the men and women who responded that day. There was hesitation, not just because of the location and the difficulty to get to the sight, but also the thought of what they would encounter once they were able to reach it. All the training in the world couldn't prepare them for that! While it was never a decision of whether or not they would go, they knew it would be difficult and heartbreaking. After all, no one could survive that kind of crash in that remote of an area!

About five hours after the original call came in that a plane had gone down, the rescue workers came upon the first few pieces of debris. In the beginning, all they came upon were suitcases strewn around, clothing that had fallen out of broken luggage and metal pieces of the aircraft. The further in to the center of the crash they got, the more bodies they found. Sadly, there were no survivors found for a while and the volunteers, along with the men in charge of the search and rescue, began to lose faith that they would find anyone alive.

~

SABRINA AND ALEX LISTENED AS THEY heard the rescue workers get closer to where they were pinned. Alex grabbed Sabrina's hand. "Do you hear that? They'll get to us soon. Hang in there."

"I'm trying but I'm so cold. I can't feel my legs."

"Don't think about that. Think about sleeping in a safe warm bed."

"Should we yell so they know where to find us?"

"Not yet. They're still too far away to hear us. Especially with the loud equipment they're using to clear the brush."

Both survivors laid helplessly waiting for the crew to get closer to them. It was agonizing knowing they were close but not quite there. Sabrina kept trying to move her legs and yet still hang onto the little girl that rested by her side. Her thoughts kept going to the sweet little face of the girl when she was standing in her mother's lap smiling through her toothless grin. It was so hard to believe that so little time had actually passed and the number of lives that were lost in that short time. There just had to be other survivors!

Alex on the other hand kept thinking about his parents. He knew they would be frantic with worry. He knew that his Dad would be the strong one for his Mom and would know what to do and who to call. He just felt so bad about the worry his parents would endure until they got word he had survived. No parent should have to think about a child dying before them. God knows they had enough to worry about these last several years with Sam and his lack of direction, which his parents constantly agonized about. Alex sent a silent prayer to the heavens to keep his parents strong until they got word about him.

~

As THE RESCUE WORKERS GOT CLOSER to the sight of the crash, they found even more bodies of the passengers. Desperately they searched under debris, in the brushes and near trees, constantly calling out in hopes of a response from a survivor. The first hour or so yielded only disappointment as body after body was found, tagged and respectfully placed in a body bag. As their spirits began to wane, the supervisor in charge of the rescue crew asked for silence. A prayer for those who lost their lives seemed an appropriate thing to do.

One of the rescue volunteers, a minister from one of the local churches, was just about to end the vigil when they heard a faint cry for help. After the third "Help, over here", a smile came upon the faces of the workers and they frantically fought their way through the debris to get to where the sound had come from.

As they came upon Alex they gently picked up the debris that was lying across his stomach and legs.

"Mister, can you hear us?"

"Yes. Be careful, there's a lady beside me that's alive too."

Another worker knelt beside Sabrina. "Can you hear me lady? Can you tell me what hurts?"

"I can't feel my legs."

"Okay, just hang in there. We have paramedics on their way. They should be here in a few minutes."

As the rescue workers worked to remove the debris so the paramedics could get to them easier, one man gently searched both Alex and Sabrina's bodies for other injuries. Eventually the paramedics made it to them and began IV fluids and worked to stabilize Sabrina and Alex for the transport out of the woods. When they tried to move the little girl that lay beside Sabrina she refused to let go of her hand.

"Please M 'am. You have to let her go."

"I can't." Sabrina sobbed. "She's all alone. I don't know what happened to her mother. I can't leave her alone here in the dark."

The minister that had given the prayer knelt down to Sabrina.

"M 'am, if you'll trust me, I'll stay with her. I won't leave her side until I know that she won't be left here in the dark. Okay?"

Sabrina hesitated briefly. "Promise me you won't leave her alone here?"

"I promise."

After a few moments Sabrina let go of the girls' hand.

FROM THAT POINT ON THE RESCUE was a hazy memory for both Alex and Sabrina. So many people surrounded them; it was hard to concentrate on a particular face. As they were jostled around in the effort to get them out of the woods, the pain became more unbearable and both survivors quietly passed out from pain and exhaustion.

Chapter 5

WHEN SABRINA WOKE UP, THERE WERE several people staring down at her. One she knew was a doctor but the others she wasn't sure. The doctor addressed her by name and asked how she was feeling. When she said that she was doing okay, another man said that he wanted to ask her a few questions. At that point a little scuffle between the doctor and the other man started until the doctor threatened to call security to escort them out. Reluctantly the men left with the threat that they would be waiting outside to speak with her.

"What was that about?" Sabrina asked.

"Those men are from the FAA and the NTSB. They have some questions for you about the crash."

"But I don't know have any information for them. I have no clue what happened."

"I understand that Miss Wallace. But they will still need to talk to you. I just wanted to fill you in on your condition. Do you feel up to it?"

"Yes".

"Do you have any relatives that we can call for you?"

Sadly Sabrina shook her head. "No. My parents were killed a while ago and they were pretty much alone except for me. If you could call my friend Katherine Manning though, I would appreciate it."

"Actually she's on her way here. As I understand it, she was making a pretty good scene at the airport in Boston trying to get information on you. When they finally found you, she took the next flight out. I imagine that she will be here very soon."

"Thank you."

"You're welcome. Now, Miss Wallace, as to your condition. You're one very lucky young lady. Both of your legs have fractures and you have three broken ribs. Your ribs will heal, as well as your legs, but it will take time and physical therapy. You'll have to be in a wheelchair for a while, and then we will try to get you up and on your feet with walking casts and eventually into therapy. It's important that you take things slowly. I have you on pain medication right now and we will wean you off slowly depending on your progress. Do you have any questions for me?"

Sabrina looked up at the doctor with tears in her eyes. "Were there any other survivors other than Alex and me?"

Sabrina watched the doctors face. A sensation of intense sickness swept over her. With one look at his face, she had her answer.

"I'm sorry Miss Wallace. You and Alex were the only survivors."

The doctor shifted uncomfortably in his white soft-soled shoes. He had a lot of experience reporting bad news to his patients over the years and prided himself on how well he handled those situations. This, however, was the most difficult. Seeing the desolation and sadness in the beautiful young woman's eyes was almost more than he could bear.

"Look, Sabrina, I can't even begin to imagine what you went through out there. It's going to be imperative that you talk about what you saw. We have wonderful grief counselors and psychologists here at the hospital. I've made arrangements to have someone come in to talk with you in a while. You need to heal, not just your body but your heart and soul as well."

Sabrina gave a half hearted nod in consent.

"How's Alex?"

"He's doing very well. He's been asking to see you."

"I would like to see him too."

"I'll let him know. In the mean time, those gentlemen need to talk to you. I know it's difficult to talk about, but they have a job to do. Do you feel that you can handle it?"

Wearily Sabrina nodded her head. Within minutes she was bombarded with questions and patiently tried to answer them as best she could. After about forty minutes of nonstop interrogation, Sabrina became tired of trying to recall the horrifying details of what she experienced. She shuddered inwardly as the memories came back. She had seen too much, witnessed too many painful scenes. Sabrina was at the point of screaming when a voice from the direction of her doorway spoke.

"I think you guys have all you need for the time being. Why don't you give her a break?"

Sabrina looked over to find Alex lounging in her doorway, his arm in a sling and a bandage on his forehead. The men questioning her grumbled but agreed to leave her alone, with the understanding that they would be back if they needed anything else. With a curt nod to Alex, they left Sabrina's room.

Alex walked over to Sabrina's bed and sat in the chair next to her. He took hold of her hand and smiled at her. "How are you?"

A glazed look of despair began to spread over her face. "There was no one else Alex. Everyone died." As Sabrina began to sob, Alex gently put his good arm around her and hugged her.

"I know Sabrina. We can't focus on that though."

Sabrina pulled away from Alex to look into his face. "How can we not? All those poor people. All those poor families. That sweet little girl!"

Alex gently shook Sabrina and looked intently into her eyes. "Because if we don't, we'll go crazy. It's too much."

Sabrina looked at Alex's eyes and watched as tears appeared and ran down his cheeks. She nodded her head in agreement and lay back down in bed. Alex tucked the blankets around her broken legs and tapped her on the shoulder. "Just try to get some rest. I'll stop in to check on you again later."

"Where is your family Alex? Do they know that you're all right?"

"Yes, they know I survived. My brother should be here any minute now and my parents later this evening. Now get some rest. I'll check in on you again later."

~

WHEN ALEX GOT BACK TO HIS room, his brother was pacing back and forth. When he saw Alex walk in he started yelling. "Where the hell have you been?"

Alex smiled at his brother. "Nice to see you too Sam."

Sam shook his head and walked over to hug his older brother. "I'm sorry. It's just that for about six hours we all thought you were dead. Mom had to be sedated and Dad just locked himself in the library. I called in every favor anyone ever owed us to try to get more information about survivors. Then I found out that there were two but they didn't have any names. That took another hour or so of bribes and I still didn't get anything."

Alex put a hand on his brother's shoulder. "Take a breath Sam. It's okay."

"Jesus, I can't even imagine what you went through. How are you? It's good to see you up and on your feet."

"I'm okay. Other than the fracture to my left arm, a few broken ribs and this bump on my head, it could have been worse. I could be dead."

With the bluntness of Alex's statement, Sam shivered. "That's something I never hope to see in my lifetime."

Alex smiled ruefully and hugged his brother again. "Me either"

Alex climbed into his narrow hospital bed and Sam pulled the blankets up. He settled into the chair next to his brother's bed. The two men sat for a long while softly chatting about what happened. Sam spoke of the help he had received in trying to get information and Alex told him about Sabrina. At times they just sat in silence simply enjoying the fact that they could be together, something that had almost been taken away.

~

SABRINA WOKE UP TO A GENTLE tugging on her arm. When she was able to focus more clearly, she saw Katherine sitting in the chair beside her bed. When Katherine saw that her friend was awake, she cried in earnest, Sabrina simply patted her shoulder and spoke soothing words to her. After a few minutes when Katherine was under control, Sabrina hugged her friend. "It's nice to see a friendly face."

"Oh God, Sabrina. I don't know what I would have done if I had lost you. How are you?"

"I'm doing okay."

"The doctor said that both of your legs were broken. Will they heal?"

"Yes Katherine, they will. With a little time and some physical therapy I should be okay. Did you call the people I was going to meet with to tell them I wouldn't make it?"

Katherine had the first real laugh she had had in a long time. "Honest to God Sabrina, only you would survive something like this and come out asking about a client. And to answer your question, I didn't. To be honest with you, I was a little busy trying to find out if you were alive. And if the client has a problem with that, he can take a flying leap...."

"I get your point Kat. Don't worry."

"I wasn't. You were."

Katherine looked at her friend closely. "I'm so thrilled to have you back. I was so scared."

Sabrina took Katherine in her arms and squeezed her tight. "I know. I was scared too."

That being said, both friends settled down for some quiet conversation, comfortable silences and an evening of simply being close. Both women knew full well just how close they had come to loosing each other. This admission was dredged from a place beyond logic and reason. God had smiled upon them and had, for some unknown reason, spared Sabrina's life.

Chapter 6

FOR THE NEXT SEVERAL DAYS SABRINA and Alex were bombarded with requests from the news media for interviews. Both of them politely declined but issued a joint statement simply saying that they were healing and sent their deepest sympathy to the families of those who had died in the crash of Pentium Airways. As the days passed stories came out in the tabloids about the crash, some true, most not true. There were interviews from some of the family members of the deceased victims one night in the news. Alex had been visiting with Sabrina when it came on. Both of them were amazed to hear the anger in the voices of some of the family members because it had been them to survive and not their loved one. Not wanting to hear any more, Alex silently got up and shut the television off.

There was still no news on why the crash had happened. Both the FAA and the NTSB were only saying that it was under investigation Nearly all of the victims had been recovered so at least the families left behind could lay their loved ones to rest. Alex and Sabrina were hoping at least that would help some of the anger that people were feeling toward them to dissipate.

Katherine stayed close to Sabrina most of the time. They would discuss business, Sabrina's health, but never anything about the crash. It was still too hard for Sabrina to face. Even the grief counselors couldn't seem to make headway with her. Sabrina just wanted to forget what she saw, not keep reliving it.

Eventually Katherine had to go back to Boston so the company wouldn't fall completely apart. Some of their clients were understanding and sent cards and flowers while others were more single-minded and only cared that their business was being put on hold. Katherine bought some supplies that Sabrina would need to continue working while she was in the hospital and left for Boston to keep the office running.

Alex, on the other hand, only wanted some peace and quiet, but couldn't seem to get it. His mother and father were constantly in his room. It seemed to Alex that the only time they left him was to catch a few hours of sleep. At first it was endearing but now Alex was becoming somewhat annoyed but didn't want to say anything to his beloved parents. They had been through so much too, thinking he was dead, that he didn't want to hurt their feelings.

Sam on the other hand was surprising Alex. He stepped right in to help with the business that, until now, he only wanted to be a silent partner in. It was a relief to have some help and after Alex checked what his brother was doing and found everything in perfect order, he laid back to heal feeling very comfortable that Sam was taking care of business. He was actually very good at it. Of course, Alex knew how smart his brother was or he wouldn't have agreed to start a company with him.

~

THERE WERE MANY NIGHTS, AFTER ALEX'S parents visited him, that they would stop in to check on Sabrina. Alex had introduced her to them shortly after they arrived at the hospital that first night. After seeing the injured girl lying helplessly in the bed and learning how she was alone, except for her friend, they developed a soft spot in their hearts for her.

Alex's parents always appeared at her door with smiles on their faces and usually some small gift to try and lift her spirits. They were such kind, loving people that Sabrina couldn't help but respond to them. There were times, though, that it made Sabrina realize just how alone in the world she truly was. There were many nights when after a visit from Alex's parents, she would fall asleep dreaming of what it would be like if her parents were still alive.

One evening after Sabrina's visitors left, Alex peeked in around the corner of her doorway. "Is it safe? Are they gone?"

Sabrina shook her head at Alex and smiled. "You're awful! They're such lovely people. You're lucky to have parents that love you so much."

Alex sauntered into the room and sat in the chair next to her bed. "Try having them hover over you. It gets oppressive."

"Try not having anyone around to love you like that. It's not as great as you seem to think it would be" Sabrina said with a burst of anger.

Alex looked into Sabrina eyes. "I'm sorry. I sometimes forget everything that you've lost in your life. I love my parents Sabrina, more than anything else in the world. It's just that since the plane crash, my parents look at me as if I might croak at any time. I don't know what to do to make them feel better. Do you believe that Mom tried to cut my meat up for me tonight? It's like I reverted to a little kid again."

Sabrina shook her head. "I'm sorry too. I didn't mean to snap at you. I just don't think that I can take much more of this hospital. The walls are starting to cave in on me."

Alex got a strange look in his eyes and stood up. "I'll be right back. Don't go anywhere."

"As if I could."

Sabrina heard Alex's deep laugh as he left her room. About half an hour later, Alex came back to her room with a wheelchair and two attendants.

"What's this?"

"Come on lazy bones. Time to get a little breather of fresh air and some different scenery to look at."

Very gently, the two attendants helped Sabrina into the wheelchair and made her comfortable with several pillows and a blanket around her legs. After she was settled, the attendants helped Alex wheel her out of the room, up several floors, and out through a set of double doors.

Sabrina smelled the fresh air first, then as she looked around, she saw a table set in one corner surrounded with several miniature trees decorated with a thousand twinkling lights. On the table, which she could now see was draped with a sheet, were beautiful flowers lovingly placed in a plastic water pitcher and two glasses nestled in what appeared to be champagne bucket. On the wall was a CD player with soft music playing. "Oh Alex, this is beautiful."

After the attendants wheeled Sabrina to the table and made sure she was secure, they quietly left. Alex sat down in the chair beside her and smiled. "I thought you might enjoy an outing. Apple juice?"

Sabrina looked at the table a little more closely. The glasses were plastic and the champagne bucket was a metal pan that Sabrina was sure she didn't want to know what it was actually used for. Inside the pan were several hospital issued containers of apple juice.

Alex smiled ruefully. "This was the best I could do on short notice. They don't allow alcohol on the premises. It was all I could do to get one of the housekeeping staff to find their Christmas decorations to do the lights."

"I think its perfect Alex. I can't believe that you went to all this trouble."

"It was actually fun. Besides, I needed out of my room too! I'd ask you to dance but under the circumstances I think it would be impossible."

"Doesn't matter. I never could dance, even with two good legs."

Alex and Sabrina spent the next two hours listening to the music and talking about anything that came to them. The conversation was easy and the silences were comfortable. That's what Alex liked about being with Sabrina. He didn't feel any pressure to fill the conversation gaps.

At one point Alex awkwardly wheeled Sabrina over to the wall to look over and see the city below. "I wonder if anyone else comes up here to the roof to get away. It's so beautiful" Sabrina said.

Alex looked over the wall, then back to Sabrina. "Do you think you'll ever fly again?"

Sabrina was startled by the question. "I haven't thought about it to be honest with you. I don't think I really want to but with my business, I don't see how I can't. Not to mention getting back home when they let me out. I don't think my legs could take that long of a drive. Besides, hiring someone to drive me all the way back could be pretty expensive. What about you?"

"I think it will be a little terrifying, but like you, my business demands it."

As they both thought in silence staring at the city below, a gentle rain began to fall. Alex smiled and started for the door to get some help in getting Sabrina back to her room. Within minutes, she was back in bed and settled for the night. Alex kissed her forehead and walked to the door.

"Alex" Sabrina called softly. When Alex turned around Sabrina smiled at him. "Thank you. That was the loveliest evening I've had in a long time."

"Me too" Alex said and turned and walked away.

That night, for the first time in a while, Sabrina slept soundly.

~

THE NEXT DAY WHEN SABRINA WAS sitting up in bed reading a book, a nurse came in and asked if Sabrina would like a visitor. When the nurse said that she didn't know who it was, Sabrina, fearing a reporter, declined to see the man.

An hour later, while Sabrina was working on one of her clients projects, she heard a noise and looked up to see a man standing in her doorway.

"I'm sorry miss. I know that you said that you didn't want to see me, but I needed to speak with you."

"Look mister. I'm not giving any interviews right now. Not just to you, but anyone. Please try and understand."

"I'm not a reporter."

Sabrina looked confused. "Then why do you want to talk to me?"

"My name is John Corbin. My daughter and wife were on your flight."

Sabrina braced herself for the anger she knew would be coming. "Look Mr. Corbin, I'm very sorry for your loss but….."

"I'm here to thank you Miss Wallace."

"Thank me? For what? I'm afraid that I don't understand."

"May I come in for a moment? I promise that I won't stay for very long. I know that you need your rest."

"I'm sorry. Please, come in and sit down."

Mr. Corbin walked slowly in and stood by Sabrina's bed. When she looked closely at him, she saw a man carrying the heavy burden of grief. Instinct made her reach for his hand. "I'm so sorry Mr. Corbin."

John Corbin simply stared at Sabrina's hand. "You have a soft gentle touch Miss Wallace. I'm glad you were there."

"Mr. Corbin, I'm afraid I don't understand."

"My daughter was the little girl you tried to help that day Miss Wallace."

Tears suddenly poured from Sabrina's eyes. "Oh my God! I'm so sorry. I tried to help her but there was nothing I could do." Sabrina put her head in her hands and cried. "I'm so sorry, I tried."

John Corbin gently touched Sabrina's shoulder to get her attention. When Sabrina looked up she saw tears in his eyes."That's what I'm trying to thank you for. I can't imagine what you saw out there, what you're trying not to remember. I just couldn't, though, go back home to bury my wife and daughter without thanking you. My daughter could have died alone out there. I'm thankful that my wife didn't have to suffer, but I have found peace in the fact that my daughter had you. The rescuers told me how you heard her and pulled her next to you to try to help her. There was warmth and gentleness in her last hours, and for that I am grateful."

Sabrina shook her head. "Somehow that doesn't sound like much."

"It does to me Miss Wallace. It doesn't bring my little girl back, but it gives me peace. God bless you for that. I hope that you heal quickly. Take care of yourself Miss Wallace. You'll be in my prayers."

"And you in mine Mr. Corbin."

John Corbin hesitated briefly before leaning down and placing a quick kiss on Sabrina's head. "God bless you" he whispered again and walked slowly to the door. Before he exited Sabrina called out to him.

"What was her name?"

Slowly Mr. Corbin turned and smiled sadly. "Hailey" he said, and then quietly left.

As Sabrina sat and thought about the beautiful little girl that lay so quietly beside her on that cold hard ground, she thought about how appropriate her name was. *Hailey, just like the comet, here for one bright shining moment, then gone.*

Chapter 7

A S THE DAYS PASSED, SABRINA BECAME more and more restless. She was tired of the hospital food, the nurses, as kind as they were, and most of all, the men from the FAA and the NTSB. There was nothing more that she could tell them and the constant questions kept bringing up things and memories that she would have preferred not to remember.

To make matters worse, Sabrina had just overheard from the nurses that the hospital was going to be releasing Alex in the next day or so. While Alex hadn't confirmed the day yet, she knew it was coming. The thought of him not being there was very difficult. She had not realized how much his presence had meant to her until she heard of his release.

It was after dinner later that night when Alex finally appeared at her door. "The nurses told me that you've been pretty temperamental today. What's up?"

"Nothing" Sabrina moodily replied.

Alex chuckled at the disgruntled tone in her voice. When he made his way over to the chair beside her bed and sat down, he smiled over at her. "Seriously, what's up? Have the NTSB or FAA guys been giving you hard time you?"

"No, that was yesterday's thrill."

"Then what it is Sabrina? Are you in a lot of pain? Do you need them to increase the pain killers for your legs?"

"No" Sabrina snapped. "I'm trying to get along without having to take so many of them."

"Okay, so what is it? Have you talked to Mr. Corbin again?" Alex asked remembering how upset Sabrina had been after he left the last time. It nearly broke his heart to hear her sobbing from down the hall. Even the nurses were afraid to go to her so knowing how close the two had become, they asked him to go to her.

Sabrina shook her head. "No. It's not Mr. Corbin. I'm fine. Really."

Alex gently took Sabrina's hand. "Look at me." When Sabrina finally looked up he smiled sadly at her. "I'm leaving tomorrow Sabrina."

"I know" she quietly whispered.

"How?"

"I overheard the nurses talking."

"I'm only a phone call away you know. If you need me for anything just call, I'll be there."

"So is this just it? We politely go back to our lives? Pretend that we didn't see everything that we saw? Never heard or felt what we did? I don't know how to be normal anymore. I close my eyes at night and I see that poor little baby. The older gentleman who just wanted to see his grandchildren again and all the other faces. I can't block it out Alex. It's too much. You're the only one who understands and now you're leaving me too."

Alex moved to the edge of Sabrina's bed and took her in his arms and cradled her gently. "I know sweetheart. Believe me, I know. And for the record, I'm not leaving *you*. Just this hospital. As hard as all this is, sooner or later we have to try to get back to normal. It's the only way I know how to make it through this. I wish that you would give the grief counselors a chance to help you."

"How can they help? They've never been through a plane crash or been one of the only two survivors. All they know is what they've learned in books."

"I know Brie, but you have to try something. You can't go on like this. It will eat you alive if you don't find some way to deal with it."

"I have to do this in my own way."

"Fine. Just start dealing with it!" Alex watched Sabrina's face then asked her, "Do you need anything before I leave tomorrow?"

Sabrina sadly smiled up at him. "No, I'm fine. But thanks."

"How about breakfast tomorrow morning? Just you and me before I leave? I'll meet you back here 8:00 am sharp!"

"Sounds great."

Alex stood up and kissed Sabrina on the cheek before he moved to the door.

"Alex" Sabrina called.

Alex turned to look at Sabrina. "Yes?"

"Thank you."

"For what?"

"For being there for me."

"We've been there for each other Brie" then Alex smiled and walked out into the hall.

~

IT WAS HOURS SINCE ALEX SAID goodbye and already Sabrina was lonely. Breakfast had been a solemn event for both of them. It was amazing to Sabrina how much she had come to rely on him. A virtual stranger up until just a few weeks ago and now she felt as if a part of her was missing.

Katherine called to speak to Sabrina about some business problems that needed to be worked out. After the business portion of the call was completed and Katherine had her "to do" list, she made several attempts at light hearted conversation. Eventually she gave up and cut the telephone call short. It was apparent that Sabrina was in no mood to talk. Katherine knew that what her friend needed now was some space to sort out her feelings. About the crash and, she suspected, about Alex as well.

The next day Sabrina tried, once again, to work with one of the hospital's grief counselors. A half hour after their session started, Sabrina wheeled out in frustration. It didn't seem to help her at all. The hard part was that this was the third one she tried to speak with but she just didn't feel comfortable opening up to any of them. Strike three, she decided. They're all out. There just had to be another way to work through this. She just needed to find out what it was!

One night, after she had eaten what resembled a piece of meatloaf for dinner, Sabrina was sitting in her wheelchair, looking out the window in her room. Feeling restless, she decided to see if she could wheel the thing around on her own. After several clumsy attempts, she began to get the hang of it and managed to get herself out her door and down the hall. Before she knew it, she was at the elevator doors. Just then the doors opened and several visitors got off. Sabrina, with a wicked grin on her face, wheeled in and waited for the doors to close. It was funny, just feeling the freedom of no one hovering over her was exhilarating. Not knowing where to go, she pushed the easiest button to reach and waited with anticipation to see where she would end up.

When the doors opened, Sabrina wheeled herself out and stopped when she heard babies crying. She looked up at the letters on the wall in front of her and read "Maternity Floor". Sabrina would have gone right back into the elevator if she could have maneuvered the wheelchair quicker. As it was, the doors closed before she could get turned around. Not knowing what else to do, she hesitated briefly, and then wheeled herself down the hall.

She passed a few rooms, and then came to a large glass window on her left. Inside she could see at least eight little babies, cozily wrapped in various pinks and blues and sleeping soundly. There were several proud parents and grandparents gazing lovingly at them. With a lump in her throat, Sabrina turned the wheelchair to leave. When she finally got a half turn accomplished, she found herself facing glass enclosed rooms on her right. Inside there were only three babies with many wires and tubes connected on them. Sabrina moved closer to the window to see them.

When one of the nurses moved a little to one side, Sabrina saw the tiniest babies she had ever seen. This evidently was the room where the sickest newborns were sent. How sad to see such tiny little humans, fighting for every breath! It made her think of Hailey and how small she seemed among all the wreckage of the plane.

After Sabrina had watched for a while, one of the nurse's came out of the room and walked over to her.

"Are one of these babies yours?"

"No. I was getting stir crazy in my room and somehow ended up here. Are those babies going to make it?"

The nurse followed Sabrina's gaze to the nursery. "We're trying, but it's still too close to call."

"What's wrong with them? Were they just premature?"

"One was. The other ones were born with a drug addiction. Their mothers used crack cocaine when they were pregnant. Now these poor babies are paying the price for their mother's pleasure."

Sabrina instantly became angry. "How could they do that? To their own children?"

The nurse smiled at Sabrina. "My name is Sharon."

Sabrina held out her hand. "Hi Sharon, I'm Sabrina Wallace."

Sharon took Sabrina's hand and smiled again. "Our crash survivor. It's nice to meet you. As to your question, the mothers are already so far into their drug problem that they can't even think of anything but where their next fix is coming from, let alone about what they're doing to their children."

"I just don't understand. Life is so precious. How could they not think of these kids?"

"You and I know how precious life is, they don't care. And you can't make them care if they don't want to. So we just do the best we can for the children."

"But how do you see what these kids go through and not get so angry at the mothers?"

"I'm too busy with the kids to think about the mothers. I used to go home after I started working in this unit and think about what I saw that day. How angry I was at the mothers. I wanted to go yell at them, make them see what they had done. It drove me mad some nights."

"So how do you deal with it now? You must have found a way. You're still here."

"Well, I had to realize I couldn't change anything first of all. Then, I found a way to try and help some of the mother's kick their drug addiction. That eases some of the anger, as for the rest, I work out at a gym. I found something that makes me feel good."

"And what about the babies here now? The mother's must not have insurance. Are the babies getting everything they need?"

"Medically, yes."

"What do you mean?"

"To take care of their health, yes, they're getting everything that they need. But for their souls, well, we do the best we can."

"You mean love."

"Yes Sabrina, love. These children need a connection, human touch. The mothers aren't capable of giving that to them. At least not now."

"So what do you do?"

"The best we can with the amount of nurses we have on duty. We hold them as much as possible, but it's not easy. These children are so sick, it's all we can do to take care of their medical needs, much less take the time to hold them and sing to them."

"It's so sad."

Just then several alarms went off showing that one of the infants was in distress. "I'm sorry Sabrina, I need to go. It was nice talking to you. Take care of yourself okay?

"You too Sharon" Sabrina whispered and slowly turned her wheelchair to the elevator doors, hoping and praying that the tiny baby would survive.

Chapter 8

THE FLIGHT BACK HOME WAS MORE difficult than Alex had anticipated. Right before he and his family boarded, a panic came over him that almost had him running to the nearest car rental agency. It took more than a few deep calming breaths before he could walk onto the airplane. It wasn't until he was back on the ground at Logan Airport that he was able to take a deep breath.

Now, sitting at his family's vacation home on Cape Cod looking out at the ocean, he couldn't get Sabrina Wallace out of his mind. She had looked so sad when they said goodbye at the hospital. He knew that she had a while before she would be released from the hospital, but where would she go to heal? Certainly her apartment in Boston wasn't conducive to someone in a wheelchair. Who would look after her? Except for Katherine Manning, there was no one else in her life.

Alex set aside his worries to look over some of the contracts that his brother had sent to him by messenger that required his signature. As he read them over a smile crossed his lips. It really was amazing that after all Sam's efforts to be the "playboy" in the family, his business sense was everything that Alex knew it would be. After this, there would be no going back for him. Alex fully intended to start taking time for himself.

If nothing else, the crash made him realize that life was much too short to waste. His business was important, but not the end all of his life. Lying in the hospital after the plane crash he realized that what he wanted most was a family of his own. He wanted that special someone that he could spend his days with. Someone to love, argue and laugh with. Funny how when he thought of that now, Sabrina's face came to mind.

Later that night, after the contracts were signed and sent back to his brother, Alex went for a long walk on the beach. He had spoken to Katherine Manning earlier and was disturbed about some of the things that Katherine had told him about Sabrina. As he walked the empty shore line, listening to the waves, he pondered all he knew about the woman who spent so much time on his mind.

First, from his own unfailing memory, she was a beautiful woman. While that alone would cause anyone to look at her again, it was by no means all there was to the woman. No, Alex thought, she had character and a kindness that went soul deep. She proved that by her actions with the little girl, Hailey, whom she tried to protect after the crash. That was probably also why she couldn't deal with what had happened. Although, if she didn't find a way to come to terms with it, Alex feared, she would never recover. I'll be damned if I'll let that happen Alex thought!

Then there was what little information Alex coaxed out of Katherine. Sabrina, in her earlier days was the great, although trying, joy in her parent's life. According to Katherine, Sabrina drove her parents crazy with one scheme after another. More often than not, her father would have to bail her out of situations. Then after their sudden and tragic death, Sabrina drew into herself and had not let anyone, other than Katherine, get close to her. She was no longer the outgoing, carefree girl and to this day, still deals with nightmares about her parent's crash.

As far as her business went, Alex had already heard of her before the crash. She was a respected and talented architect and her clients appeared to be very pleased with her work. Her reputation was solid, even with the most difficult clients, and she was earning more than enough for a comfortable life style. Most likely, at the rate she was going, she would be a wealthy woman before much longer.

As Alex was headed back to the house, his mother intercepted him. "Alex, I wanted to have a word with you."

Alex put his arm around his mother's shoulders and continued walking. "Sure Mom. What's up?"

"I've been thinking about Sabrina."

"Seems to be going around" Alex mumbled.

"What?"

"Nothing. Thinking about what?"

"When is she getting out of the hospital? Have you heard yet?"

"No, I haven't. To tell you the truth, I don't think it will be any time too soon. Her injuries were pretty extensive, but I think it will be longer because of her state of mind. So far she's gone through at least three counselors that I know of and no one seems to help."

"Why do you think that is?"

"She's not ready. I don't think that she ever really recovered from her parents' death, and then this happened. I think that her mind is on overload. She's protecting herself by not facing what happened. Unfortunately, she's not sleeping, she rarely eats and the doctors are concerned. I'm worried too. When I spoke to her last night she sounded so disoriented and lost. I don't know what to do to help her."

"Why do you think that you're able to handle what happened and she can't?"

Alex thought about the question for a few minutes before answering. "Because of you and Dad and Sam. I'm not alone. You guys are my safe haven."

"Maybe that's what Sabrina needs too" his mother calmly stated.

"So what do we do Mom? She's too old to be adopted" Alex joked.

"Not necessarily."

"Meaning?"

"Meaning I think that we should have her come to stay with us here. We could hire a nurse to live in for a while. The house has bedrooms on the ground level so getting her around with the wheelchair won't be a problem. And to be honest, she seems stronger with you around her. Any other problems we can deal with as they come up."

Alex stopped walking and turned to his mother. "Do you think that Dad would mind?"

Alex's mother smiled gently up at her son. "Now just who do you think came up with this plan?"

"I should have known."

"Your father is a loving, kind man. Even though he prefers that not everyone know it."

Alex hugged his mother close. "Thanks Mom. I'll call Sabrina and talk to her about it."

"A word of advice Alex. Sabrina is a very independent woman. She's learned over the years not to depend on anyone, much less let anyone to get very close. Don't give her a choice."

Alex nodded at his mother's wisdom and made his way into the house to place the call to Sabrina.

~

AS SABINA LAY IN HER HOSPITAL bed, thoughts of the little babies upstairs weighed heavily on her mind. Life could be such a cruel experience. She alone could attest to that fact. Those poor babies, however, were so innocent. It was unthinkable what they were going through just trying to get from day to day, let alone breath to breath.

As her thoughts jumped from one thing to another, the doctor in charge of Sabrina's case came in to her room.

"Do you have a minute Ms. Wallace?"

"I'm a captive audience Dr. Stone. Literally. What did you want to talk to me about?"

Dr. Stone sat in the chair next to Sabrina's bed and looked at her intently. "Your progress, physically, is coming along fine. I think that perhaps it's time to talk about moving you to an extended care facility. There are some very good ones in this area. I could recommend a few and you could call and set up some appointments to talk to them. Unless, of course, you would like me to handle that for you."

Sabrina looked at Dr. Stone with disbelief on her face. "Why can't I just be released? And what do you mean by "physically" I'm fine?"

Dr. Stone moved uncomfortably in the chair. "I mean Ms Wallace, that there are some significant reasons why you should not be on your own at this point and time."

"Such as?"

"Well, for one thing, I can't possibly release you when there is no one to help take care of you at home. I know you have a secretary but you need a little more help than she can provide. Not to mention the fact that you have done absolutely nothing to try and deal with what happened to you. Quite frankly, I'm concerned about your mental health. You're not eating, you sleep very little and when you do you wake up with nightmares."

Sabrina looked sullenly off into space. After a few minutes without conversation she turned back to look at Dr. Stone. "Do I have a choice?"

"You always have a choice Sabrina. This isn't prison. We can't force you to do anything you don't want to do. As your physician, I'm telling you that, in my opinion, this is the option that would best suit you. I just want to try and help you."

"Thank you for your honesty Dr. Stone. I'll think about it and let you know tomorrow. Is that soon enough?"

Dr. Stone stood up and patted Sabrina's hand. "There's no rush Sabrina. We'll talk again tomorrow."

After Dr. Stone left, Sabrina laid back with tears in her eyes. The thought of going to another hospital atmosphere instead of home depressed her greatly. While she could ignore her doctor's suggestions, she knew that she was in no shape to handle things in her apartment even with a hired nurse. Unfortunately that left her precisely where she didn't want to be, still in a hospital environment. So now what?

As Sabrina sent back another dinner tray, barely touched, she struggled with the decision of what to do. While she was contemplating picking up the telephone to throw against the wall out of frustration, it rang startling her.

"Hello!" she nearly shouted into the receiver.

"Not having a good day I take it?"

Sabrina smiled into the phone. "Oh Alex, It's wonderful to hear your voice. How are you?"

"Fine. How are you?

"Fine."

"Liar. I heard your tone of voice. What's up Brie?"

"Nothing's up. Just the normal hospital blues. How's the weather on the Cape?"

Alex, hearing the shakiness in Sabrina's voice, wouldn't let the matter drop. "What's wrong Sabrina?"

After a few minutes of silence, Sabrina sighed. "Dr. Stone wants me to go into an extended care facility. I need to let him know tomorrow. I guess they've done all they can for me here."

"What do you think about that Sabrina?"

"I hate it but I also know that it's probably the right thing to do. At least for a while."

"What if I gave you an alternative?"

"What are you talking about" Sabrina questioned.

"What about coming to Cape Cod?"

Sabrina sat silently in her hospital bed not comprehending what Alex just said. After a few minutes of silence Alex finally decided to break into her thoughts. "Sabrina? Are you still there?"

"Yes."

"So, what do you think" Alex impatiently asked.

"I think that you're crazy. I can't possibly stay with you."

"Why not?"

"Do you want the top ten reasons or the entire list" Sabrina questioned.

"Think about it Sabrina. Most everything here is ground level so getting you around isn't a problem. Mom, in her usual panicked parenting style, hired a nurse to live here for a while in case I croak, so medically there's no reason why you can't come here. She may as well earn the money Mom's shelling out. As for your business, working here isn't a problem. We have everything you need; besides, you've been working from your hospital bed for a while anyway and doing it well. As for anything else, we can deal with it as it comes up."

"What about your parents Alex? How would they feel about it?"

"As much as I would like to take credit for this idea, it was theirs so that takes care of that question. Look Sabrina, you could probably come up with a million little details to worry about. For once, why don't you just give in and go with it? Stop over analyzing and just say yes."

Sabrina closed her eyes and holding onto the receiver, laid her head back. It would be so nice to be with people who seemed to truly care about her instead of the polite coolness of another medical facility. Not to mention the fact that she would be near Alex again. It seemed that the only time she felt safe anymore was around him. But could she impose on people that she truly just met?

As Sabrina contemplated another team of doctors and nurses prodding and poking and trying to force her to "face" things, she came to a decision. "If you're sure about this Alex, I would love to take you up on your offer."

On the other end of the line Alex was smiling. "Finally, a good decision!"

Chapter 9

ALEX WAITED AT THE AIRPORT TERMINAL for Sabrina alone, except for the live in nurse, who accompanied him to help. Knowing the flight would be difficult, he didn't want anyone around to witness her distress, so he asked the driver he hired to wait at the exit door. It seemed an eternity before her flights arrival was finally announced. Slowly the airplane came to a stop at the terminal and passengers began filing out on to the tarmac. When everyone else was off the plane, an employee of the airline and the hired nurse took a wheelchair to assist Sabrina from the plane. As Alex watched with concern, a pale and shaky Sabrina emerged.

Alex looked to the nurse who silently shook her head. As she walked up to Alex, she informed him that according to the stewardess, Sabrina had a difficult time. "They said she was terrified during the flight. She's in a lot of pain too."

"Can you give her anything" Alex whispered?

"I tried. She refused."

Alex shook his head to indicate understanding and walked over to Sabrina and knelt beside her wheelchair. "Hey Champ. How are you?"

Sabrina looked into Alex's eyes and weakly smiled. "Depends. Am I on the ground yet?"

"Would I be next to you if you weren't?"

"You have a point there." Sabrina grabbed Alex's hand. "Please tell me that you've opted to drive to the Cape and not put me on a tiny plane."

Alex put his arms around Sabrina and squeezed her tightly. "I wouldn't do that to you Brie. I have a car waiting just outside. You'll be okay."

As the two survivors held on to each other, a local newspaper started snapping pictures of the two of them. When Alex realized what was going on, he stood up, glared crossly at the surrounding group of photographers and motioned for the nurse to help wheel Sabrina away from prying cameras.

After about twenty minutes, Sabrina was settled in the back seat of the car with her legs stretched out on the seat and a pillow neatly tucked behind her. The nurse sat next to Alex, facing Sabrina, and kept a watchful eye on her.

"By the way Brie, I'd like you to meet Betty. She's the nurse Mom hired to look out for both of us for a while."

"It's nice to meet you Betty" Sabrina said.

"It's nice to meet you too Sabrina. Anything you need, all you have to do is ask. I'm here to help you get better."

Sabrina pondered the gray haired lady and thought her age to be about 70. She had a smile that showed kindness and strength and Sabrina instantly warmed to her.

"I appreciate your willingness to live in and help me out. I'm not very demanding I promise."

Betty smiled at Sabrina. "Well now, you need to help me earn my money so please, ask me for anything. I'm not one to like sitting around so you need to rely on me as much as you need to. Besides, the more I can do to help you now, the quicker you will be up and feeling better."

"Thanks Betty."

As the driver negotiated the exits from Logan Airport, Alex reached over to Sabrina and took her hand, holding on to her for comfort. Like a life line to a drowning victim, Sabrina held just as tightly to him.

As the miles passed them by, Sabrina looked around with interest. "I didn't realize how much I missed this place."

"I know what you mean. I didn't think that I missed it either until I came back. I need a few directions on where your apartment is. Katherine will be waiting for us. She's supposed to have everything you need ready isn't she?"

"Yes. I spoke to her yesterday. She'll have everything ready. Are you anxious to get back to the Cape?"

"Not really. I just wanted to get you settled. I'm sure you're tired."

Sabrina directed Alex's driver to her apartment and, true to her word, Katherine was waiting outside. After the car stopped, Sabrina opened the back door and Katherine reached in to hug her friend. Pulling back slightly, Katherine stared into Sabrina's eyes.

"How are you?"

Sabrina smiled gently. "The flight was a little shaky but I'm okay. How are things here?"

"Great. All clients seem satisfied. I've only had to put out a few fires, but nothing for you to worry about. I think I have everything you need together. I'm hoping to drive down to the Cape this weekend to check in on you. If there's anything we've forgotten I can bring it to you then."

"I appreciate everything you're doing for me Kat. I know it's been rough on you too. Hopefully I'll be up and on my feet soon and things can start to get back to normal."

The two friends spent a few more minutes visiting as Alex and the driver packed the items in the back of the car. When they were all done, the girls hugged each other tightly and said goodbye.

The rest of the drive passed in relative silence. Sabrina occasionally nodded off to sleep but any jolt of the car hitting a bump brought her painfully awake. Several times Alex saw her wince and tried to get her to accept a painkiller. Sabrina refused, wanting to be awake and alert when she saw his parents again. It just wouldn't look very lady like to be drooling all over herself when she greeted them.

As the car pulled into a long curving driveway, Sabrina looked around to admire the place where she would be recuperating. The house sat nestled among four weeping willow trees. The lawns were neatly manicured and boasted of hydrangea bushes vibrantly blooming in colors of lavender and blue along the front of the house.

As the car came to a stop near the front door, Alex's parents rushed out to meet them. Elizabeth and Joseph Deluca were the epitome of a married couple. What little Sabrina knew of them from their short visits at the hospital, they seemed like the perfect match. Elizabeth was petite, soft spoken and graceful but very definitely the anchor that held the Deluca family together. Joseph Deluca was tall, distinguished and spoke with a voice that commanded respect. When Sabrina had first met him she was rather intimidated by him, but after just a few short minutes, she realized that while his voice was loud and stern, he was a gentle man with a huge heart.

In a flurry of activity Sabrina was helped from the car and into the wheelchair, hugs were exchanged and she was wheeled into the house to get settled. Alex patiently stood by as his mother fussed over Sabrina.

Elizabeth Deluca took great pride in her dream house by the water. As she wheeled Sabrina from room to room it was evident that she had designed this house with an open, airy feel combined with a hominess that made a person want to just kick their shoes off and stay a long time. The color scheme she picked throughout the downstairs rooms was the palest aqua and the furniture was cream with accents of a deeper aqua marine color. With an architect's eye, Sabrina fully understood the time and effort that went into every detail of this house. She took great pleasure in what she saw and admired the taste of the kind woman showing her around.

"Oh Mrs. Deluca, this is such a beautiful home."

"Please Sabrina, call me Elizabeth. And thank you. It was always a dream of mine to design and have this house built. It took a while but I love spending time here."

"I can see why. It's stunning."

"Let me show you where your room is. Obviously I have you here on the ground floor. Alex's room is next to yours and Betty will be across the hall. I know you can't go upstairs yet but Joseph and I are upstairs and we have three other guest rooms up there as well. All the bedrooms are obviously to your left. If you turn right off the living room you'll find the kitchen and dining rooms are there."

Elizabeth wheeled Sabrina into the room she would be occupying.

"I hope you like your room."

Sabrina looked around her temporary new living quarters. The walls were painted a soft cream color with pictures accenting the colors of red and burnt orange. There was a queen size bed with the same oranges and reds in the designs on the comforter and throw pillows. There was a dresser against one wall and a chair with an ottoman near a sliding glass door that faced the ocean. Against another wall was a doorway that led into private bathroom and another door that was a closet.

"I hope you'll be comfortable. If there's anything you need, just let me know."

"Thank you so much for taking me in."

"Believe me, it's my pleasure."

Alex came up behind his mom and put his hand on her shoulder. "I think we should let Sabrina rest before we have dinner later."

"Absolutely! I'm sure she's exhausted from her long journey. I'll ask Betty to come in and get her settled. Do you need anything else dear?"

"I'm fine, but thank you."

Alex waited for Betty to come in to see if she could use any help getting Sabrina into the bed. As it turned out, Betty was very strong and more than capable of taking care of her patient. Within minutes she was settled on top of the comforter with a blanket over her legs and a pain killer in her system. Alex closed the curtains to block out the sunlight and turned to Sabrina.

"All set?"

Already close to dream land Sabrina nodded sleepily. "Thanks Alex."

"Sweet dreams Brie."

LATER THAT EVENING, AFTER SABRINA WOKE from her nap and freshened herself up, Betty took her into the living room where Alex and his parents sat having a drink and talking. As she wheeled into the room, it was Joseph who got up to get her a drink.

"What can I get for you my dear? Juice, soda, wine, what's your pleasure?"

"I think I'll just have a diet soda if you have it."

Joseph smiled down at Sabrina. "You women and your diet sodas. I say if you're going to have a soda just go for it. None of this mamsy pamsy stuff. Besides what can you possibly have to worry about with your size?"

Sabrina smiled up at the kind man handing her the soda. "Thank you. I just want to make sure that bad choices don't catch up to me later in life."

Alex watched the playful banter between his father and Sabrina. It was evident that his parental unit was taken with the younger woman. It seemed that his father looked at Sabrina as the daughter he had always wished for. Joseph and his sons enjoyed their fair share of rough housing but his father always said his mother needed a girl to help tame the wild men in her life. It just seemed so natural to have this young woman sitting in the house he spent so much of his life in, interacting with his parents. Briefly Jessica came to mind and Alex realized that he could never imagine her being comfortable in this same situation. What came so naturally to Sabrina and the ease he felt with her interacting with his parents was definitely not a part of the brunette's DNA. Jessica could be harsh and abrasive when she wasn't the very center of attention and looking back, Alex had always been on edge wondering what she might say that would leave him in a position that required him to apologize or explain. This was definitely a much nicer way to pass time and Alex was beginning to realize that he just may have dodged a very serious bullet!

After a short time Elizabeth went into the kitchen to finish preparing dinner. Alex and his father passed the time discussing the local neighbors, who was at the Cape for the summer, who was in the middle of a nasty divorce and whose child was caught in a compromising position. Sabrina, amused by the conversation, listened intently.

Elizabeth announced that dinner was ready and Joseph Deluca wheeled Sabrina into the dining room. A simple dinner of baked chicken and rice was served by Alex's Mom, followed by a light dessert of strawberry shortcake.When everyone had their fill, Alex suggested they all go out to the patio.

"Thanks dear but I'm going to do the dishes. Why don't you and Sabrina head out. You're father's going to help me with the dishes then we'll join you okay."

Sabrina watched as Joseph reached over to touch his wife's hand and smile into her eyes. Silently they got up from the table and started picking up the dishes. Touched by their show of affection Sabrina turned toward Alex who was also watching his parents. As his mother walked over to get Alex's dishes, she ruffled his head and leaned down to kiss his cheek.

"Get going you two. You're in my way."

Alex got up from his seat and awkwardly wheeled Sabrina out to the patio. With his one good arm and help from Sabrina, they were settled in short order facing the panoramic views of the Atlantic Ocean.

"This is so beautiful Alex. This must have been a wonderful place to grow up."

"It was after all the construction was completed. One summer Mom insisted on being here when they were nearing the end of construction. She wouldn't leave and she wouldn't stay at a hotel so Dad rented this trailer for us to stay in. I figured if we could still like each other after living in such close quarters we'd always be close. Don't misunderstand, we had our spats and arguments but at the end of the day things always seemed to work out."

"For some reason I imagine it wasn't quite that easy" Sabrina smiled.

"There were some bruises and a few brotherly punches but eventually it all worked out. Although I do recall at one point after a particularly loud argument Sam decided to teach me a lesson and he climbed up this tree to hide. I thought he had run away because of a fight we had about some girl. I looked everywhere for him. I walked up and down the beach frantically calling his name. Eventually I had to head back to the trailer and confess to Mom that Sam had run away because of me. She just smiled and told me to go in the trailer. When I walked in Sam was sitting at the little pull out table eating a peanut butter and jelly sandwich, happy as a clam. He told me he was up in a tree and watched me the whole time. When I walked down to the beach he jumped out of the tree and went in for lunch. I was so mad at him that I punched him in the arm as hard as I could. He started crying and Mom came running in and sent me to bed for hitting him. To this day I swear he played right outside the window where my bed was just to torture me."

Alex's parents walked out onto the patio. "You always felt so responsible for Sam and he used that against you, you know."

Elizabeth settled herself opposite her son and smiled. "He loved making you feel guilty for the smallest things. You fell for it every time Alex."

"So why didn't you stop him Mom. Show him the error of his ways?"

"I intervened when it was necessary. You two needed to find you own way in the relationship. Besides, look at you now. Both great men and you have a company together. What more could a mother ask."

"Oh I don't know Mom, one less tortured youthful soul back then?"

"You weren't so tortured Alex. Besides, if you'll remember, you gave as good as you got most days! So tell me Sabrina, what was your childhood like?"

"Mom....I don't think......."

"It's okay Alex. I don't mind talking about it." Sabrina turned to Elizabeth to answer her question. "I was a very lucky girl growing up. I didn't have a sibling like Alex to torture but I was really happy. My parents were kind and loving and they doted on me terribly. We didn't have a house on the water like this but we spent a lot of time at the beach. We went mostly to Newport Rhode Island. Mom loved going to the beach then walking around all the shops in town. One time we did this murder mystery train ride. It was a lot fun."

"Did your mom work Sabrina?"

"She didn't work until I was old enough to go to school. Even then she only worked part time in the town library. My Dad was an attorney and had his own firm in Boston before he passed away."

"Donald Wallace was your father" Joseph exclaimed.

"Yes, why?"

"I've met him before. He worked on a case that involved a friend of mine.They were being sued for some ridiculous reason and your father took the case and cleared them of all wrong doing. Steve, the guy your dad helped, was so thankful. Your dad did a great job for them! Funny, small world isn't it!"

Sabrina smiled. "Yes, it is. You said that you met him?"

"Oh, I did. After they won the case in court Steve took your Dad out to lunch. I happened to walk in the restaurant at the same time to grab some lunch and they asked me to join them so I did. Your dad struck me as a very kind, professional man. Something about him though told me he wouldn't be the type of attorney that I would want against me in a court room. Steve told me later that he could be tenacious when he needed to be."

"I've heard that as well. I only saw the other side of him but during their funerals a lot of his colleagues were there. During the luncheon afterwards they told a lot of stories about him and some of the cases they dealt with. It was interesting to hear about a side of my dad that I never saw. He tried not to bring his work home with him so Mom and I got the kinder, gentler Donald Wallace."

Sabrina's voice faded away in thought as she looked out over the ocean. As the silence continued, each person deep in their own thoughts, Alex watched Sabrina's eyes close and her head start to dip. Elizabeth must have seen her as well because she quickly suggested that it had been a long day and perhaps it was time to call it a night.

Betty was called to help get Sabrina settled for the night. As she wheeled her from the patio both Elizabeth and Joseph stood up and kissed Sabrina's cheek.

"Sleep well Sabrina. Get some rest."

"Good night. And thanks again for letting me stay here."

Betty wheeled Sabrina into her room and together they ironed out a routine that worked best for both of them in getting her teeth brushed, hair combed and ready for bed. Alex hovered nearby in case any help was needed. After Sabrina was settled into bed and a pain killer administered, Betty left her patient in the capable hands, or hand in this case, of Alex.

"Do you think you can sleep now" he asked.

Sabrina smiled sleepily. "I think I can. I feel like I've been going for days."

"Do you need anything before I head to bed myself?" Sabrina shook her head.

"Okay, I'm right next to you so if you need anything at all just call me okay?"

"I will. Thanks Alex, for everything."

Alex kissed the top of Sabrina's head. "You're welcome. Good night."

Chapter 10

ALEX WAS AWAKENED BY THE GENTLE shaking of his shoulder. When he opened his eyes he realized that it was still very dark outside. He looked at the clock on the night stand beside his bed and saw that it was only 2:00 in the morning.

"Alex wake up" his mother whispered.

"Mom what's wrong, are you okay?"

Just then he heard soft moaning coming from Sabrina's room.

"She's been moaning and crying in her sleep for a little while now. I came down for some juice and heard her. I didn't know whether I should go in myself or wake you. I figured maybe you should go in since she's more comfortable with you. Maybe I should wake Betty."

"No, I'll go in Mom. Let Betty sleep."

Alex pushed his covers back and swung his legs over the side of the bed. He padded over to his door and out into the hallway. His father was pacing back and forth in front of Sabrina's door. With a look of relief he patted Alex's shoulder and opened the door for him to enter.

Alex quietly walked over to Sabrina's bed so he didn't startle her and gazed down at her. She was thrashing around, the covers twisted around her casts. He turned and walked over to switch on the soft light at the opposite end of the room from where Sabrina was sleeping.When he walked back to her bed he saw that tears were streaming down her face and she was moaning saying something about her being too little. Alex assumed she was dreaming about Hailey, the little girl she held on to the night their plane went down.

He carefully sat on the edge of Sabrina's bed and lightly touched her shoulder. Sabrina let out a loud scream and sat straight up in her bed looking around wildly. Alex spoke softly to her to try and calm her down. Sabrina was shaking uncontrollably but finally calmed enough to look into his eyes. It took several seconds before she realized that it was Alex sitting with her. When it dawned on her that he was truly there, she just hung her head and wept. Alex silently put his good arm around her and drew her to him. Not meeting any resistance he pulled her closer to him and simply held her while she cried.

Alex's parents watched from the hallway as their son held the tortured woman in his arms. It was heartbreaking to see the two of them, each dealing with the grief and sadness that seemed to overcome them when faced with the tragedy of the plane crash. Not knowing what else to do they simply put their arms around each other and walked back upstairs to their room. They both knew that the only thing that could help those two was time to heal, a loving family and each other's support.

Alex held Sabrina for a while until her sobs lessened. Eventually she pulled away and looked at Alex and apologized for causing him to lose sleep. Alex just shrugged his shoulders and reached over to get her a Kleenex from the box on her night stand.

"Are your dreams usually this bad?"

"Actually that one wasn't as bad as they usually are. I'm sorry Alex. I didn't mean to upset you. I was hoping that I was tired enough that it wouldn't happen tonight."

"Do they happen every night?"

"Usually. Sometimes I dream of Hailey. Sometimes I see the smoke before the plane went down. Sometimes I dream of those people on the news that were so angry that their loved one wasn't a survivor and we were. What about you Alex, do you have dreams? You always seem so in control."

"I have dreams too Brie. It's hard not to. I think we both experienced some pretty awful stuff. I don't think mine are as frequent or as bad as yours because I've been able to open up about it. Honestly, you really need to find someone you can talk with. Very few people have experienced a plane crash so you'll never be able to find a counselor with those qualifications if that's what you're looking for. There are plenty of very smart, capable, professional people that can help if you would just let them."

"I know."

"Brie......" Alex cradled Sabrina's cheek with his good hand. "I wish there was a way that I could make this better for you."

"Me too" Sabrina whispered.

Alex looked into the most beautiful aqua blue eyes gazing back at him. Eyes that a man could truly get lost in. Slowly, without really thinking, Alex leaned forward and pressed his lips to Sabrina's. He pulled back, all too quickly for Sabrina's liking, and apologized. Sabrina simply cupped his face with both hands and pulled his face closer and kissed him more thoroughly. Tentatively at first, Alex touched her lips with his tongue. Sabrina opened her mouth in invitation and the kiss quickly ignited a passion that both of them felt deep in their souls. Both giving as much as taking, both completely lost in the feel of being together.

Reluctantly Sabrina pulled away from Alex before things progressed much further. Not an easy thing since all she wanted to do was get lost in the warmth and safety of this wonderful man.

"You should get some sleep Brie. Why don't you lay back and close your eyes."

"Alex, would you mind staying with me for a while until I fall asleep?"

"Of course." Alex stood up and walked to the other side of Sabrina's bed. He sat down on the bed so that the right arm, which wasn't casted, was next to her. He settled his back against a few pillows and motioned for her to move closer. Sabrina scooted over and put her head on his chest and Alex wrapped his arm around her shoulders. They lay together in a comfortable silence until eventually Sabrina's breathing slowed and she drifted off to sleep.

Alex laid awake thinking of the kiss they had just shared. He had known for a while now that he was physically attracted to her but the kiss just magnified those feelings.

Just what I don't need right now Alex thought to himself. Life at this moment was complicated enough without adding in a relationship. There was so much to get settled before his head would be clear enough to consider anything like that. First in line to think about was Sam. He was doing a great job at stepping up and taking care of things but just what did that mean? Was this a temporary thing until Alex was recovered or did Sam intend on becoming a true working partner?

Alex was afraid to hope that this change in Sam wasn't temporary. It would be so nice to have someone to share the burdens of running the investment firm with. At first it seemed like a good idea to have Sam as a silent partner. Alex could be in charge, call all the shots and do things exactly how he wanted them done. As the business grew and became more demanding, it was evident that there was too much for one man to handle alone. In fact, Alex was planning on approaching Sam on the idea of hiring a VP to take some of the load off him. The sacrifice of his relationship with Jessica, while in retrospect was a good thing, was a high price to pay. Alex always wanted to have that special someone to stand by him and he wasn't getting any younger. He still wanted that in his life and he wanted to be young enough to enjoy it!

Funny how in thinking of that special someone Sabrina came to his mind. As hard as it was, he needed to consider any ramifications being in a relationship with her could bring. As attracted as he was to her, she just wasn't in the right frame of mind to think about a relationship. There was so much weighing her down at the moment that getting involved would only add to her burdens. Or possibly even give her an excuse not to deal with what had happened. Better to give her the space to focus on what was most important right now. Alex knew full well that if she didn't figure things out now, she had no hope at a healthy, loving relationship.

Eventually Alex's mind began to get fuzzy. He was having a difficult time focusing on any one subject when his eyelids drooped and he fell asleep with Sabrina in his arms.

THE NEXT MORNING SABRINA WAS AWAKENED by the sound of seagulls playing outside. She looked over to see that her window had been opened. Wondering who had opened it, she threw the covers back and gently swung her casted legs over the side of the bed. She sat there for a few minutes, waiting for her equilibrium to settle, and thought about the previous night. She wondered how long Alex had stayed with her. Lying in his arms last night she felt so safe. And that kiss! Remembering it brought a blush to her cheeks. What a kiss! Now that would be a wonderful way to end each night!

After a few more blissful moments remembering the night before, Sabrina decided it was time to get the day moving. Facing Alex would be a little embarrassing but she better get to it before she lost her nerve and stayed in her room the rest of the day. Nice as it was to have him, leaning so heavily on another person always made her uncomfortable.

Sabrina looked over at her wheelchair and quickly realized that she was going to need help. It was just too far away from her bed to chance reaching for it. Just as she was about to call for help, Betty breezed in the door with a smile on her face and a cheerful greeting. In short order she helped Sabrina get ready for the day. In no time at all she was bathed, dressed, medicated and being wheeled out to breakfast.

Alex's parents were already sitting at the table eating a simple breakfast of fresh fruit, bagels and coffee when Sabrina was wheeled in. Betty placed her on the side of the table where the chair had been removed to allow for the wheelchair. At the same time, entering from the kitchen door, Alex came sauntering in balancing his bagel plate on his coffee mug with is good arm. Sabrina glanced at him quickly then lowered her eyes to her hands clasped in her lap.

Seeing her discomfort, Joseph Deluca quickly intervened. "So how are you doing this morning Sabrina? Were you able to get back to sleep?"

With that comment Sabrina realized that they both must have witnessed her nightmare. Feeling ashamed and guilty at having awakened them from their sleep Sabrina apologized.

"Nonsense" Mr. Deluca explained. "Don't even think about it. I'm usually up a few times during the night anyway."

"What can I get you for breakfast" Elizabeth asked, steering the conversation to a less touchy subject.

"I'll just have some fruit and coffee."

"Coming right up."

Elizabeth filled a bowl with fruit and poured coffee into a mug and handed it to Sabrina. The conversation around the breakfast table was pleasant and ranged from the weather to the headlines in the Herald. Alex and his father bantered back and forth on the viability of a company that was being auctioned and Sabrina, listening intently, realized that Alex was quite the businessman.

OVER THE NEXT SEVERAL DAYS A comfortable routine was established. Between Betty and Alex's parents, Sabrina was easily maneuvered through the house, nap times adhered to and medications dispensed. Most times against Sabrina's wishes but Alex would not allow pain to become a factor in her recovery. As frustrating as it was when the drowsiness began to take effect from the medications, the easing of the pain was a blessing.

Alex and Sabrina were sitting out on the deck watching the sun go down. The view from where Sabrina sat each night was breathtaking. There was nothing like the sound of the ocean waves and the view that could sooth Sabrina's mind. Sitting here each night with Alex sitting close to her brought a sense of peace that she found elusive during the long nights.

Alex looked over to Sabrina and smiled. "I'm heading in to grab a drink. Can I get you anything?"

Sabrina looked back at Alex. "No, I'm fine. But thanks."

As Alex stood up he reached his hand over and rubbed his fingers gently over Sabrina's cheek. When he came back out a few minutes later with his drink he sat down and glanced again at Sabrina.

"So tell me about your adventure when you came up missing that one day at the hospital. Where did you go?"

"How did you know about that…..did you have spies everywhere?"

Alex chuckled. "No."

"You make it sound like I was gone a long time. It was a few hours and I never left the hospital. Although the temptation was definitely there."

"Where did you go Brie?"

Sabrina hesitated for a moment before confessing. "I ended up at the nursery. When I got myself onto the elevator I pushed the closest button which happened to be the maternity ward. The doors closed before I could get back in so I just went forward. I ended up talking to a nurse who worked there handling the really sick babies. There were children there whose mother's were addicted to drugs while they were pregnant. Now their children are addicted. It was so sad Alex, those poor innocent children. The nurses are so busy trying to take care of their immediate medical needs but those sweet babies need human touch. They need to be held and soothed, and they're just not getting that on a regular basis."

Alex gently took Sabrina's hand in his and held it. "You shouldn't have gone up there Brie. You've been touched by too much sadness lately."

"But something should be done Alex. Those babies need so much more than they're getting."

"Why don't we tackle getting you on your feet again first?"

"You're saying let it go?"

"I'm saying one step at a time. Concentrate on getting well, get your bearings then decide what you can and cannot handle."

Sabrina stared moodily out at the ocean. She knew Alex was right but it was hard thinking of first Hailey and then the babies she had seen. So many children, so much sadness. Sometimes it seemed like laughter and happiness was something that belonged to others in the world and not her.

Chapter 11

FRIDAY WAS QUICKLY UPON THEM WHICH heralded the arrival of Alex's younger brother Sam. While Sabrina had been introduced to him briefly at the hospital after the crash, she really hadn't had a chance to get a feel for who he was. From what Alex had told her, he played as hard as Alex worked which from Sabrina's point of view, was a waste and colossally unfair to Alex!

In the late afternoon Sabrina was resting on the deck facing the ocean when she heard Alex's mother let out a scream. She turned her wheelchair around as quickly as she could to see her caught up in the arms of a blond headed man with a huge grin on his face. Sam she decided loved to make an entrance.

Eventually Mrs. Deluca was released only to be pulled into his embrace again and a sound kiss planted on her cheek. His mother gently cupped Sam's cheek and smiled into his eyes. The love between parent and child was so evident that it brought tears to Sabrina's eyes.

Joseph Deluca came in through the kitchen munching on an apple and saw his younger son grinning down at his wife.

"Well, the prodigal son returns I see."

"Dad, you just saw me a few weeks ago. You make it sound as if it's been years," Sam said with a smile.

Joseph walked over and hugged his son. Not a distant manly touching of the shoulders or a handshake but an honest to goodness tight hug from a father who loves his son.

"Good to see you son. How was the drive? Catch any traffic on the bridge?"

"Nope, my timing was pretty good. Where's Alex?"

"He's in the den making a few phone calls."

"Doesn't he ever just relax?"

"He should be done shortly" his Mom said. "Why don't you go out to the deck with Sabrina? I'll grab a few snacks and your Dad and I will meet you out there. What do you want to drink?"

"Anything is fine. Thanks Mom. I didn't have time for lunch so I'm starved."

"When aren't you" she said with a gentle smile.

Sam headed out towards the deck where Sabrina was sitting watching them. As he came closer Sabrina smiled a welcome and turned her chair to face the ocean. Sam shut the screened portion of the sliding door and scooted a chair over next to her facing the ocean.

"Hello Sabrina. How are things going?"

"Good Sam. It's nice to see you again."

"You too. Is my brother taking good care of you?"

The sliding door opened again and Alex walked out. "Of course I am. Do you think I'm a slouch?"

Sam stood up and embraced his brother. He pulled another chair on Sabrina's other side for Alex to sit and smiled at his brother. "You're looking better than the last time I saw you. How's the arm doing?"

Alex briefly touched Sabrina's arm as he sat down then looked at Sam. "Better. Hopefully I'll get the cast off next week then I'm good to go."

The two brothers conversed for a while until Elizabeth came out to the deck with a tray of drinks and snacks. Everyone settled around the patio table under the big umbrella and got caught up on each other's lives. The easy rapport that the Deluca family enjoyed was evident in the light teasing they each endured. Old family stores were brought up, each one meant to embarrass either of the two boys. All stories evidence of a family that was very tight knit, but one that had weathered the bad times more easily because they had each other.

At one point Sam was teasing Alex about being a one armed bandit with his arm in the sling and all the hilarious excuses he could use for a short time to get sympathy from people. As Sam's comments became more ridiculous Alex and his parents just sat back and let him go, each enjoying his quick wit and easy humor.

Eventually their parents got up to pick up the leftover food and Sam and Alex settled in to discuss the business. Sabrina enjoyed quietly watching the two brothers bounce ideas off of each other. Sam would bring up an issue that had arisen, Sam would give his opinion and Alex would either agree or give another thought on how to handle things. It quickly became clear to Sabrina that Alex knew full well his brothers abilities when he had started the company with him. She gained a whole new respect for Sam, now knowing that there was so much more to him than the playboy exterior he showed. Inside him was a quick, bright mind that complemented Alex's abilities. Together, the brothers would go far.

At some point Sabrina must have nodded off in her chair because she came awake when her head jerked down. Alex took a hold of her hand and smiled at her.

"You look tired Brie. Why don't you lie down for a little while before supper?"

"I hate that I still get so tired but maybe I should."

Betty came out to wheel Sabrina in to her room. Between her and Alex she was settled comfortably in no time. Betty closed the curtains and left the room. Alex sat on the edge of her bed and took her hand.

"You okay?"

"Just tired."

"Try and get some sleep then. I'll check on you in an hour so."

"Thanks Alex."

Alex leaned over and, not bothering to fight the urge, gently kissed Sabrina on the lips. "You're welcome."

~

LATER THAT NIGHT EVERYONE HAD SETTLED back out on the deck once again. Joseph Deluca was grilling steaks with both Alex and Sam standing on each side giving him instructions on how they thought it should be done. Sabrina and Elizabeth were sitting at the table watching the grill battle in progress.

"Seriously Dad, you should put a little vegetable oil on the grill before you put the steaks on" Sam advised.

"I like to have the steaks just thrown on. You don't need oil" Alex complained.

"This from a man who has to have his Mommy cut his meat for him."

"Only because of this damn cast and you know it" Alex barked.

"So you say" Sam joked.

"Now boys, I've been grilling steaks without your advice for years now. I think I can handle this on my own. Why don't you both go sit and leave me to it!"

"Fine but when they start to stick to the grill don't complain to me."

With that Sam plopped himself down in the chair next to his Mom. Alex followed suit and winked at Sabrina as he sat next to her.

"So Sabrina" Sam began, "tell me about your business. Alex says that you're a pretty good architect."

Sabrina looked over at Alex and smiled. "I do pretty well I guess."

"Do you know that building in San Francisco next to Fisherman's Warf near our client's office" Alex interjected.

"The one you incessantly mention every time you come back from there? I remember it."

"That's Sabrina's design."

Sam sat up straighter in his chair."Seriously, that's you?"

Sabrina smiled. "It is."

"Well I'm impressed Sabrina. You're very good."

"Thank you Sam. It took me a while to get the design how I wanted it but I was happy with the result."

"As you should be. I'm not that inclined to architecture but I know when something looks good and even I can see how that building stands out in comparison to everything around it. Very impressive indeed."

Sabrina smiled her thanks and listened as the conversation turned to questions on how Alex's extended family was doing. It seemed they had quite a few aunts, uncles and nieces and nephews. They discussed who was doing what, who was visiting whom and generally just getting caught up on family life.

Dinner and the rest of the evening passed in a relaxed and happy mood. Sabrina felt very blessed to be around these warm, easygoing people. To be able to just relax and enjoy their company was very special to her. Of all the places she could be, she was grateful to be with them and felt warmed to her soul. A feeling she hadn't had in a very long time!

$$\sim$$

LATER THAT NIGHT BETTY WAS HELPING Sabrina get settled in bed when Alex's Mom walked into her room. When Betty left them alone she sat on the bed and took Sabrina's hand.

"How are you doing dear? You seemed particularly quiet this evening."

Sabrina looked at Elizabeth with a smile on her face. "Everything's fine. Just tired. I was enjoying sitting back and listening to the conversation. Your family seems so close.

"I really hadn't thought about it but I guess we are. There are those moments when somebody doesn't get along with someone else but we usually do a pretty good job of working our way through that stuff. I admit it doesn't always get solved as quickly as it should but that's what happens when you have so many different personalities in one family."

"You and Joseph have done a wonderful job raising Alex and Sam. Both boys are so smart and warm and caring."

"It was more difficult when they were younger. The boys were so different. I think the hardest thing as a mom was to not get involved with every little squabble they had. I always wanted to charge in to fix things."

"It's funny how they are so close and yet so different. Sam is easy going and funny while Alex is more quiet and intense but very strong. I don't think there's anything he couldn't handle. He's a very special man."

Elizabeth glanced out the bedroom window then looked back at Sabrina. "You see exactly what Alex wants the world to see. Don't get me wrong Sabrina, he is very strong. But Alex had a difficult childhood."

"In what way?"

"Look, I don't want to betray Alex but you should know that there is more to him than the tough business man. When he was younger he was watching Sam for us one day. They had walked to the park just down the street to play for a little while. Alex was walking Sam home for lunch an hour or so later. When they got back they were surprised by a burglar already in the house. I guess the guy panicked because he charged at the boys with something in his hand. Alex threw Sam behind him and took the brunt of the beating. To this day I don't know what scared the guy enough to make him stop but he ran out of the house and Sam called 911. Alex was in the hospital for over a week and it took a good six months before he could sleep in the house again."

"That's awful" Sabrina whispered. "Poor Alex!"

"I didn't tell you this to show him pity. He'd hate that. It's just that he feels things so deeply but doesn't talk about them. The plane crash is another thing. He's talked to a counselor about what happened and I think that truly helped him. He won't talk to us about it though. He's very careful not to burden anybody with his thoughts and feelings. To be honest, I wish he would but that's just Alex. Even when his girlfriend broke things off, I know he was hurt but he won't talk about it. He holds everything in but stubbornly encourages everybody else to lean on him."

"I see what you mean. We went through the same thing during the crash but he makes it seem as if he's doing better with things. I guess that's not necessarily true."

"It's hard to guess. While he may not talk to us about it, unlike you, he has spoken to professionals" Elizabeth kindly mentioned.

"Touché" Sabrina smiled.

"You better get some rest now. I've talked your ear off." Elizabeth tucked the blankets around Sabrina and kissed her on the top of her head. "Good night dear."

"Good night. Sleep well."

Elizabeth stood up and smiled down at Sabrina then walked out of the bedroom.

~

A FEW MINUTES LATER ALEX WALKED in to say good night to Sabrina. He sat down on the edge of her bed and took her hand in his. For several minutes they simply looked at each other.

"You looking at me like you're trying to see into my soul" Alex laughed.

"Just trying to figure you out."

"What's to figure out? We've been practically living in each other's pocket for a while now. You should have me all figured out by now."

Sabrina squeezed Alex's hand. "I just think there's more to you than I know. I'd like to understand what makes you tick."

Alex looked uncomfortable under Sabrina's direct stare. He shifted a few times then leaned over and kissed her on the forehead. "You should get some sleep Brie. I'll see you in the morning okay?"

"Alex…….." Sabrina began.

Alex looked into Sabrina's eyes for a few minutes then slowly leaned in. Sabrina met him half way and gently touched her lips to his. After a few brief seconds Alex took Sabrina's head in his hand and deepened the kiss. His tongue parted her lips and what began as a light kiss became a raging inferno. Alex couldn't get close enough to Sabrina. He shifted closer on the bed to her as both their tongues dueled and their breathing became heavier.

Shaking himself, Alex moved away from Sabrina with regret in his eyes. "Jesus, I'm sorry Sabrina. I shouldn't have done that."

Sabrina grabbed Alex's hand before he could pull away. "Alex, please, I wanted that to happen as much as you did."

"But it shouldn't have. You're still recovering and I just don't think this is a good time to start a relationship."

"But Alex....."

"Get some rest Sabrina. I'll see you in the morning."

With that he quickly exited the room without even looking back.

Sabrina lay back against her pillows. Geez that man could kiss!! His sense of being proper was frustrating though. She may be in a wheelchair but that didn't mean she didn't feel things. Being near Alex could be very dangerous to her peace of mind. It seemed a constant battle between trying to keep her independence and distance and wanting to curl up in his arms.

~

ALEX WALKED OUT OF SABRINA'S ROOM and quietly shut the door. He was in deep trouble! It took everything he had to pull away from her.

He walked out onto the patio for some fresh air and to ponder the dilemma of how to keep some distance with Sabrina when he was so drawn to her. As he was standing looking out over the ocean his mother quietly came up behind him.

"You look so sad standing here Alex. What's wrong," his mother asked.

"Nothing."

"Sabrina getting to you," she smiled at him.

"No."

"Hmmmmmm.....a man of few words. Which means I'm right and you don't want to talk about it."

"Mom" Alex began.

"Just be careful Alex. I care for Sabrina and I don't want to see her hurt. She's been through a lot in her life. I don't think she can take much more pain right now. As for you, I love you more than I can find the words to tell you and I don't want to see you hurt either. I want you to be happy Alex. Just promise me you'll be careful. For both of your sakes."

"Don't worry Mom. It's fine."

Elizabeth looked skeptically at her son, lightly touched his arm in support then turned and walked back in the house.

Alex thought about what his mother had said. She certainly didn't bring up anything that he hadn't already thought about. The attraction he felt for Sabrina was just getting stronger with each passing day. She was vulnerable but beneath that he could see that she was the type of woman he always thought he wanted in his life. Someone with a sense of who she was, professional with a career of her own so that he wouldn't feel guilty for the long hours he put in, and someone who wouldn't rely on him to feel "completed". Whatever the hell that was. Some line from a movie that never made any sense to him. One person needing another person to feel completed. What a load of malarkey!

Which still brought him back to the dilemma of his feelings for Sabrina. Just how should he go about handling them?

Alex looked out over the water for a while then impatiently rubbed at his eyes. Well, since the answers didn't seem to be coming so easily, might as well head to bed and sleep on it. Things always seemed easier and better in the light of day.

Silently he walked back in to the house, paused outside Sabrina's room for a few seconds before he pushed open her door. He walked over to her sleeping form and gazed down at her face. Even in sleep she was frowning over something that was playing on her mind. He wished he could say or do something to erase her worries. Such a beautiful woman with so much sadness.

Alex pulled the covers up closer to Sabrina's chin, touched her hair softly then walked from her room.

Chapter 12

SATURDAY MORNING ALEX, SABRINA AND SAM were sitting on the patio enjoying a lively breakfast. Alex and his brother were constantly poking at each other which to Sabrina's delight included a few digs at her. It seemed that when Sam was around no one was safe from being the brunt of one of his jokes.

Just as they were finishing up Katherine popped her head around a bush by the steps leading up to the deck.

"Anyone home?"

Sabrina squealed in delight. "Katherine, you're here!"

"I was here a while ago but no one was answering the door. I started to walk back to my car, heard the laughter and headed back here. Hi Alex," she said as she spotted him sitting next to Sabrina.

"Hi Katherine. Come on up. Sorry we didn't hear you. My parents went out on some errands and sitting back here I didn't hear the door."

"No problem." Katherine finally noticed the other man sitting at the table. Flashing a brilliant smile in his direction she looked him up and down and purred "Well hello to you stranger."

"Down Kat. It's just Alex's brother."

"Ouch" Sam laughed. "Just his brother......not very flattering Sabrina."

Sabrina looked sheepishly at Sam. "Sorry about that. I didn't mean it in a bad way."

Sam stood up and reached his hand out to Katherine. "Hi. I'm Sam, just the brother. And you are?"

"Katherine Manning. Just the assistant."

Sam chuckled at Katherine as she continued to hold his hand and stare.

"Nice to meet you Katherine. Can I get you some breakfast? Coffee?"

Katherine realized she was still holding on to his hand and smiled then let go. "Sorry about that. I would love some coffee if you don't mind."

"No problem."

Sam went into the house to grab her coffee and smiled to himself. There was hope for this weekend after all. Just when he thought he would be stuck watching Alex and Sabrina making goo goo eyes at each other all weekend, in walks Katherine and life just got a little more interesting.

With coffee in hand and a few extra muffins in case she changed her mind, Sam headed back out to the deck. He placed the coffee in front of her and sat down. "So how long are you staying Katherine?"

"Just long enough to go over some work details with Sabrina. I'll probably head back in a while."

"Ah, come on. Why don't you stay overnight? We have plenty of room and besides, I'm sure that Sabrina would love to have a familiar face around for a while. Face it, she's been stuck with Alex's mug for weeks now, it would give her a break."

Alex quickly chimed in. "You really should Katherine. Sabrina would love the company and it's a perfect weekend to be at the beach."

Katherine looked to Sabrina for guidance. Sabrina smiled at her friend and shook her head to indicate a yes. She was about to answer when Sam had a thought.

"Unless of course you have a boyfriend to get back to?"

Both Katherine and Sabrina busted out laughing. Sam and Alex looked at each other in confusion. "What was so funny about that?" Sam asked.

"Oh if you only knew," Katherine said through her tears.

"Knew what?"

"Let's just say that Katherine hasn't been having much luck in the dating arena lately." Sabrina interjected.

"Luck" Katherine squealed. "I've been in dating hell for a while now. I'm officially through with that whole scene. I've decided that I would rather sit home alone and become a crazy cat lady before I go out on another blind date. Men suck. No offense, gentlemen."

"Oh, none taken" Alex smiled.

Within minutes Katherine had them all laughing as she described some of her more recent disastrous blind dates she had gone on. From the man who still lived with his mother and discussed how he meticulously trims her toenails for her to the accountant who actually still owned a leisure suit and wore it on their date. They laughed about her description of the man who had seriously long hair growing out of his ears to the man who had no teeth.

"Yes" Katherine said softly as the laughter died down. "I'm done. I just can't take the disappointment anymore."

At that moment Elizabeth and Joseph arrived back home from their errands. Introductions were made and Sam mentioned how they had asked Katherine to stay the night.

"We'd love to have you stay Katherine. We have plenty of room" Alex's Mom said.

"Thank you Mrs. Deluca. I would love to stay if you're sure."

"It's Elizabeth and we'd love to have you."

"Well" Alex interrupted. "Why don't we leave these lovely ladies to handle some of their business?"

"Maybe we can take a swim later Katherine if you want" Sam said when he was close to the door.

"Actually I would, but I didn't bring my suit. I wasn't planning on staying."

"Well, when Sabrina's through being a task master I can run you down to the local store and we can grab a suit and anything else you need for the night."

Katherine smiled her pleasure. "That would be great. Thanks."

Alex leaned down to whisper in Sabrina's ear. "Do you need anything before I head in?"

Sabrina smiled up at Alex. "No, I'm fine."

"How's the pain? Need anything?"

"No, but thanks."

"Okay" Alex kissed the top of her head and followed his family back inside.

~

AFTER THEY ALL EXITED KATHERINE TURNED and looked at Sabrina. "Okay Brie, what gives?"

"What do you mean?"

"Where do I begin? We can start with how you are feeling. Then you can tell me about your buddy Alex who watches you like nobody's business and lastly and most importantly you can tell me about his seriously hot brother."

"Well, first I'm feeling pretty good, given the fact that I feel like a complete invalid, I'm sick of this wheelchair and I'm about to go completely out of my mind. As for Alex I can't figure him out yet and as for Sam just be careful."

"I get the first part. I know this is hard for you, especially relying on other people. Just hang in there. Your physical therapy should start soon and hopefully that will be the beginning of getting you back on your feet. Be patient Brie. Not too long ago I thought I had lost you! Tell me about Alex."

Sabrina sighed. "I don't know Kat. He confuses me. He's so strong but gentle with me. Very caring, always checking to see if I'm okay or need anything. He looks at me and I just feel warm all over. He kissed me the other night, a really passionate kiss that was just about the best thing I've ever felt, then he backs away and apologizes. Not very good for my ego I can tell you. This morning, he's back to the distant but caring man. I just don't know what to make of him."

"Brie, you need to give yourself, and him, a little break. You've both been through so much. It's just going to take some time to work your way through all this stuff."

Sabrina looked over at her friend. "Thanks Kat. I've missed you so much. I've needed your calm, objective thoughts."

"Glad I could help. Now......tell me about gorgeous Sam. Why do I have to be careful?"

"Oh Kat, he's such a nice man. Just be careful. He's known as sort of a playboy. I don't know what's true and what's rumor. I'd heard of him before I even met Alex and it was mostly about the girls he's been around with, his party life. Stuff like that. Then I meet him and I get a completely different feel from him. Just be careful okay?"

"I will. I promise."

Katherine then pulled out her briefcase loaded with work and for the next several hours they made their way through a back log of business issues that needed to be taken care of.

~

AS THE CAR PULLED INTO THE local store's parking lot, Sam looked over at Katherine and smiled. "I think we'll be able to find everything you need here."

"Sorry to take you away from things back at the house. I really could have gotten myself here."

"Please, I needed the break. Between Mom and Dad hovering over Alex and Sabrina and those two doing the whole "romance dance" I needed to get away for a few."

Katherine chuckled. "The "Romance Dance?""

"You know the whole watching each other thing but not wanting the other one to know they're watching thing. The sly glances hoping to not get caught looking. The longing looks at each other. Yuck!"

"What, you're not a romance kind of guy" Katherine asked.

"It's not that. I just think that if you're interested in someone you should just come out and tell them. See where it leads. Stop wasting time on the stupid stuff that doesn't matter."

Katherine looked over at Sam in disbelief. How sad that he's so determined to brush off the most exciting part of a new relationship. The anticipation, the longing, the excitement of the newness of getting to know someone.

Shaking her head she just laughed. "Come on Mr. Downer. Let's get this shopping done so we can get back. Personally, I like watching the Romance Dance!"

~

SEVERAL HOURS LATER ALEX AND SABRINA were sitting on the patio watching as Katherine and Sam horsed around on the beach. It was a beautiful Saturday with clear blue skies and a gentle breeze blowing. The sound of laughter as the two of them ran into the waves and dove into the water brought a smile to Sabrina's face. It was good to see her friend relaxing and enjoying herself. Katherine had certainly been pushing herself to relieve Sabrina of as much of the work load as she could to give her time to heal. She deserved to enjoy herself. In fact, she deserved so much more in her life including finding a man who would take care of and appreciate her for who she was.

Sighing, Sabrina gently laid her head back against the lounge chair that Alex and Betty had settled her on and smiled.

Alex reached over and touched Sabrina's hand. "You look peaceful. What are you thinking?"

Sabrina looked once more out to the ocean and watched as Sam picked Katherine up and threw her into the incoming wave. Hearing her come up laughing brought another smile to her face.

"Just that they sound so happy. It's nice to hear so much laughter. We're very lucky to be here. To see and smell the ocean, this gorgeous day."

Alex looked out at his brother playing in the ocean. "I agree with you Ms. Wallace. We're extremely lucky. I'm glad you realize that. I was beginning to wonder."

"That's a mean thing to say Alex. I know how lucky I am to be here. To be alive. Why would you say something like that?"

"Because I just don't know how to help you Sabrina. You won't open up to anyone, your nightmares aren't going away and you just seem to be running away from what happened. You need to face this head on so you can get your life back."

"Who made you the expert on how I'm supposed to handle this? Just because I don't handle things like you doesn't mean that I'm not trying. I'm doing this the best way I know how Alex. I'm sorry if it's not fitting in to your personal time table."

"I didn't mean it like that Brie. I'm just worried about you and......."

"Hey you two, why so serious" Sam called.

Alex and Sabrina looked over to see Sam and Katherine standing on the steps leading up to the patio with towels around their necks looking worried. They were so caught up in their argument that neither of them realized they were no longer alone.

Alex stood up and walked to the other side of the deck running his hand through his hair in frustration.

Sabrina looked up at Katherine. "It's all good" she smiled, although not convincingly.

Sam looked over at his brother and shook his head. "Well, Kat and I were just thinking that it would be fun to play a little Pictionary. What do you think of that?"

Alex turned towards Sam and simply raised his casted left arm.

"Give me a break Alex. You're right handed."

"Okay, how about the fact that I can't draw?"

"You and Sabrina can be partners. As an architect I'm sure she can carry you on her back in the drawing department. Come on! It'll be fun. Kat and I are going up to go change, grab the game and some snacks and we'll be right back. Get your game faces on!"

Katherine looked at Sabrina with her head cocked to one side in question. Sabrina just smiled and shook her head. "It's fine. Go change and we'll be ready."

As the two departed to get ready Alex walked back over to Sabrina and sat in the chair beside her lounger. He gently picked up her hand and looked into her eyes. "I'm really sorry Brie. I didn't mean to upset you."

"I know. It's okay. I just need some space. It'll be okay. I promise."

"You don't have to do this all by yourself. You don't always have to be strong on your own."

"Look..... Alex.....I'm here relying on you and your family. This is already way more than I'm comfortable with. Please, I'm begging you, let it go for now."

Alex ran his knuckles over Sabrina's cheek. "Fine, I'll let it go. For now."

~

ELIZABETH AND JOSEPH WALKED OUT ON to the patio to the sound of Sam and Katherine's laughter and Alex and Sabrina's disgruntled complaining.

"Hey, that's cheating. You can't draw a person's private parts in Pictionary can you" Sabrina whined.

"The rules don't say anything about any private parts. Exaggerated or not" Katherine looked over to Sam and they both cracked up laughing. With tears in her eyes, she looked back to Alex and Sabrina. Trying to control her laughter she said, "It only says that you can't use symbols." Katherine looked over to Sam for confirmation and they both started laughing so hard that they had tears running down their faces.

Sabrina looked to Alex for help. "Well isn't that a sort of symbol?"

Alex, looking amused, leaned over to Sabrina and patted her arm. "Give it up Hon. I think they beat us."

Sabrina threw her pencil down on the table and pouted. "Well I want a rematch with clearer rules. Better yet, a game with people who don't cheat."

Elisabeth walked over and patted Sabrina on the shoulder. When she looked over to a pink cheeked Katherine trying to hide the offending drawing under the game board she just smiled. She glanced at Sam and shook her head with a smirk on her face.

Sam looked sheepishly at his mother. "Now Mom, I wasn't the one who drew that."

"Give it up Sam" his father laughed. "Your mother and I both know the kind of influence you have on poor unsuspecting women like Katherine. Poor girl didn't stand a chance when you became her partner. If I was here I could have warned her."

Sam threw his hands up in the air. "I give up. Even when I'm completely innocent I still get blamed. If you'll look clearly you'll see the pencil is in her hand….not mine! Besides, we're so far ahead of those two that they didn't stand a chance anyway!"

Laughing Alex stood up and headed over to the patio doors. "I'm going to go grab something to drink. Can I get anybody anything?"

After taking a few drink orders he headed in to the house and Elizabeth sat down in his chair. "I thought we'd just order take out for dinner tonight. What sounds good to everybody?"

After discussing the merits of pizza versus Chinese food they all decided on sending Sam and his father down to the local take out place for clams and chowder. An hour later they were all back on the deck enjoying the food the guys foraged for and the ocean view as the sun went down.

Life just didn't get any simpler than this Sabrina thought. It was so hard to believe that not long ago, sitting on that notorious flight, she wasn't even sure she would live to see another day and then to realize how desperately she wanted to! How confusing especially comparing that feeling to when her parents died and she didn't want another day to come. Oh the ups and downs that life hands you! One would think you would at least get a manual on how to deal with this confusing thing called life she smirked.

"Tired Baby" Alex leaned over and whispered.

Hmmm….baby….I like the sound of that Sabrina thought. She looked over to Alex and smiled. "I hate to admit it but I am pretty tired."

"I'll get Betty and we'll get you in to bed."

Sam and Katherine watched as Alex and Betty hovered over Sabrina getting her back in to the house. Sam looked at Kat and smiled that knowing smile.

Chapter 13

AS AUGUST TURNED INTO SEPTEMBER, ALEX and Sabrina relaxed in to a routine that was comfortable. Alex's Dad stayed at their home near Boston through the week but came to the Cape house every weekend. Elizabeth stayed with Alex and Sabrina to help Betty with everything.

Katherine and Sam tried to come to the Cape whenever possible, although Kat came more often to confer with Sabrina about some of their more difficult clients. Considering the difficulties of running a business from a wheelchair, things seemed to be going relatively smoothly. Sabrina was very grateful that her reputation was established before the accident happened. She knew full well that if she were an unknown architect just beginning her practice her clients would not have waited for her.

Glancing nervously at the clock Sabrina checked her hair and started wheeling her chair from her bedroom to the living room. Her physical therapy was beginning today and she was a little nervous. Alex had gone back to Boston for the day to do some work and left her to face this on her own. Not that he could have done anything if he was here but Sabrina liked knowing he was near. Having gotten his cast removed the previous week, there really was no reason for him to stay with her 24/7. But she wanted him here dammit!

Now that wasn't a good thought!! Becoming too dependent on anyone was not a good idea Sabrina lectured herself. Sooner or later life would have to get back to normal. Which meant that Alex would move on with his life and she would have to do the same.

~

WHEN ALEX PULLED IN TO THE driveway of the Cape house, he was feeling relieved to get back. He got everything accomplished at the office that he needed to but he worried about Sabrina while he was gone. Alex was just getting out of his car when his mother walked up to him.

"Hi Mom! What's with the welcome party? Miss me?"

"Oh Alex...." his mom started.

Alex looked at his mom's face and saw the tears in her eyes. Gently grabbing her shoulders he looked at her. "What's wrong Mom?"

"It's Sabrina."

Alex's heart fell through his stomach. "What's wrong" he panicked.

"She's okay I think. It was the physical therapy. It really hurt her Alex. I could hear her cry out a few times. When I went in to check on the guy working on her he said it was to be expected. Oh Alex, I didn't know what to do. Betty was beside herself and said it shouldn't hurt like that. After about twenty-five minutes we couldn't take hearing her any more so we went in and forced the guy to leave. Sabrina was crying but wouldn't let us near her. Betty tried getting her to take some pain medication but she won't take anything. Alex I don't know what to do."

"Where's Betty now?"

"She's trying to get a hold of the doctor to discuss what happened and to see if we should take Sabrina somewhere."

"Good. I'm going in to see Sabrina."

Alex rubbed his mom's back to give her comfort then walked past her and into the house. As he got closer to Sabrina's room he could hear her sniffling. He pushed her door open and walked in to the room.

Sabrina looked up and all Alex could see was the pain radiating from her eyes. He rushed to her bed, sat down next to her and pulled her into his arms. "Ah baby..." he whispered. "What did he do to you?"

Sabrina slumped limply on Alex's chest and wept. It took a good ten minutes but eventually she got herself under control. "I'm okay Alex. I think I must have a very low pain threshold" she sniffed. "I tried to do what he wanted me to do but it hurt so much. I want to get better, I really do. I tried so hard."

With that Sabrina leaned harder on Alex and cried some more. He patiently held her until she was through and pushed her away from him slightly. "Why didn't you talk to Betty or take the pain meds she tried to give you?"

"Because I just want to get better and not rely on that stuff. I hate that I'm relying on everybody so much. I hate it Alex and I'm sick of feeling this way. I need my independence back!"

"Baby I understand what you're saying but you have to be patient and take it a step at a time. And I don't care what that jackass says, physical therapy shouldn't hurt like that. If you weren't so stubborn you would have known it too! He was only supposed to work with you to strengthen your upper body until the casts come off. Did he do more than that?"

"He had me trying to do some things using my legs. He said it was important to at least start strengthening them too."

There was a light tap on the door and Betty entered the room. She walked over to Sabrina with a stubborn look on her face and forced two pills and a glass of water into her hands. "I'm giving you two choices missy. Take these on your own or by God I'll hold you down and force them down your throat myself. What will it be?"

Alex tried to keep from smiling and looked at Sabrina to see her reaction to the threat. Sabrina blinked a few times then willingly put them in her mouth and swallowed.

Betty took the glass back, softly touched Sabrina's cheek, harrumphed a few times and exited the room mumbling something about stubborn women and their stupidity.

"I wouldn't press her again if I were you" Alex smiled.

"I guess not."

"Okay, I want you to lay back and get some rest. I want to go talk to Betty and find out what the doctor said. And for the record...that physical therapy idiot won't come near you again. Got it?"

Sabrina lay back on her pillow and smiled up at Alex. "Got it. Thanks Alex."

"Sleep. I'll be back in a few to sit with you." Alex leaned down, brushed a strand of hair from Sabrina's eyes and kissed her on the lips. "It'll be okay Brie. I promise."

~

OUTSIDE IN THE HALLWAY BETTY AND Elizabeth were pacing back and forth. When Alex came out of the room Elizabeth rushed to Alex and grabbed his arm. "How is she?"

"She's resting now Mom. Betty, what did the doctor say?"

"He said that PT shouldn't have hurt her like that. He told me to make her take those pills I brought in and make sure she sleeps. He wants to see her at the hospital tomorrow afternoon so he can remove the casts, do some x-rays and see where we are. He wants to make sure that no further damage was done by that guy. He's calling in to the physical therapy place to register a complaint on the guy. He said he wouldn't be practicing on anyone else if he has anything to say about it. The order for PT specifically stated upper body only."

"Good. Thanks for taking care of that. In the mean time I'm just going in to sit with her for a while."

Alex looked over at his mom and saw the worry in her eyes. "She's okay mom. Don't worry."

~

Sabrina was sitting with her legs stretched out across one side of the limousine that Alex hired to take her to the hospital the next day. On the opposite side was Alex, his mom and Betty sitting anxiously side by side. Sabrina looked over at them amused.

"Stop worrying. I'm fine. Really! I had a good night of sleep last night and I don't feel that awful pain that I did yesterday when that guy from the PT place was working on me."

At the mention of the guy from yesterday Alex's face grimaced. If he ever finds out the guys name and where he lives Alex planed on making him one sorry guy for what he put her through yesterday. Of all the stupid, inept…..

"Alex, stop it" Sabrina sighed.

"What?"

"I can tell by that scowl on your face that you're thinking of doing that guy bodily harm. Leave it alone."

"You're being too nice I think, but fine. I'll leave it alone."

The rest of the ride to the hospital was pretty smooth. The traffic to Brigham and Women's Hospital in Boston was surprisingly not too congested. When they arrived Sabrina was whisked up to an examination room where they were going to remove the casts and x-ray her legs.

It took several hours but eventually Sabrina was sitting up on a bed in a private room when Alex was shown in. He immediately pulled a chair next to her bed and grabbed her hand.

"How are you doing" he softly asked.

Sabrina squeezed his hand. "I'm okay. Where are your Mom and Betty?"

"They went to the cafeteria to grab a bite to eat. So what now?"

"I'm just waiting for the doctor to review the x-rays and come talk to me."

"Scared?"

"Not really. I'd rather know how things are and where I go from here. Better knowing than worrying I think."

"Good point."

Just then the door opened and a gray haired man with a white coat came into the room. He walked over to the side of the bed and held out his hand with a smile on his face. "You must be Sabrina Wallace. I'm Doctor Moore."

"It's nice to meet you Dr. Moore. Betty has said some very nice things about you."

Dr. Moore looked at Sabrina with a twinkle in his eye. "Betty used to work with me when I first became a doctor. I was scared of her back then. I hope she's treating you well. She can be a bit of a bully when she wants to get her way."

He looked over to Alex and reached out to shake his hand. "I'm Alex Deluca. A friend of Sabrina's."

"Nice to meet you."

Smiling he turned towards a monitor mounted on the wall and began scrolling through the screens. "Let's look at your x-rays now."

After locating what he was looking for and spending a few minutes combing over them he turned to Sabrina. Taking the blanket off her legs he poked and prodded around where the broken bones were. After asking her questions and having her move her toes and checking her reflexes he scooted back in his chair and smiled up at her.

"Well Ms. Wallace, things look really good. You have feeling in your legs and your reflexes are good, no sign of any infection and the alignment of the bones are perfect. To be honest I couldn't ask for better progress. I can't explain what happened yesterday with your PT guy because my orders were clear on not using your legs yet. He must have tried manipulating them in a direction that he shouldn't have or applied pressure where he shouldn't have. Who knows? From everything I see you look great and what happened didn't cause any damage."

"That's a relief. Now what happens" Sabrina asked.

"Well, now we recast your legs but with walking casts. I want you to use crutches to help as you start to get back on your feet. I'm serious when I tell you to use them. Put as much weight as you can on the crutches and let them bear your weight. I have a different PT place that I want you to use and remember to start slowly. The key is not to overdo it."

"How long will I need to have the walking casts on?"

"We'll schedule to have you come back in three weeks and take another look. Sabrina, I know that you're probably anxious to get through this but you need to be patient and not push. I feel certain that you'll be good as new but only if you listen to what I'm saying."

"Thanks Dr. Moore. I promise I'll be good and listen to what you're telling me."

He shook both of their hands. "Good. I'll send the nurse back in to get you re-casted and I'll see you back here in three weeks."

Relief shone in Sabrina's when she looked over at Alex. A nurse came in to take Sabrina to another room to put the walking casts on. Alex went out to find his mother and Betty to let them know what was happening. By 4:30 that afternoon they were all on their way back to the Cape with a smiling Sabrina and a shiny pair of crutches.

~

ALEX SAT ON THE DECK WITH his chair facing Sabrina smiling as she attempted to move around on her crutches. It was slow going but she was so happy to be able to stand, even for a short time that no one wanted to rush her.

They all had a quiet dinner together then Elizabeth went up to her room to read. Betty disappeared to her room leaving Alex and Sabrina alone sitting on the deck.

"So how are you feeling Sabrina?"

"Excited with the forward progress, tired from all the excitement."

"I'm glad."

"You seemed kind of quiet tonight during dinner. Everything okay?"

Alex looked over at Sabrina and decided to bite the bullet. "I have to go out of town on business for a few days."

Sabrina looked over at Alex. "When do you leave? How long have you known?"

"I knew when I came back yesterday. I didn't say anything because of all that happened. I also decided that whether I went or not depended on how today went. I wouldn't go if you needed me here. You know that right?"

Sabrina looked off towards the ocean thinking about Alex leaving. "I know Alex. It's fine. We have to get back to normal life sooner rather than later, right? Besides, I'm up and on crutches now and a little more self sufficient. When do you leave?"

"Tomorrow afternoon. Sam's going with me so I think between the two of us we can get done what we need to pretty quickly. We'll fly to Atlanta for a few days, meet with our clients, and then head back as quick as we can. Hopefully it will only be a two day trip."

Sabrina looked over to Alex startled. "Fly….you're getting on a plane?"

Alex took Sabrina's hand and smiled at her. "It's a little too far to drive there and back Brie. It's what I have to do. I can't let the crash stop me from being able to run my business."

"Aren't you afraid?"

Alex hesitated briefly before he let go of her hand and looked off to the beach. "Honestly, I am a little worried. I think anybody who went through what we did would feel the same way. I think it's natural. But I have to do this and better to face it now rather than put it off any longer."

"I understand." Sabrina clumsily stood up with the help of her crutches. "I'm pretty tired Alex, I'm just going to head to bed."

Alex started to get up to help her but she put her hand up to stop him. "I'm fine Alex; I can make it in on my own. I'll see you in the morning."

"Sabrina……….." he started to say but stopped when she shook her head and made her way to the door into the house.

"Goodnight" she whispered.

"Goodnight Brie."

Alex stayed out on the deck for a while thinking about the look on Sabrina's face. He understood her concerns but this was something that he had to do. He absolutely needed to get some normalcy back in to his life. Some distance from Sabrina would be a good thing too. He was very confused about his feelings for her. On one hand they had developed a very close relationship. The bond between two survivors of a horrible accident was very strong and made complete sense. On the other hand whenever he touched her he felt something so deep that it worried him. It was unlike anything he felt when he was with Jessica or any other woman for that fact. She wasn't ready to deal with what happened and until she did, there was no way he could see that they would be able to move on.

Besides, when they got back to their separate lives who knew if the attraction he felt for her would dissipate. Was it only because he felt protective of her because of their ordeal? Because he understood what she was feeling? Or could he really have feelings for her and could they have a future together?

Yes, Alex thought, some time away from her to get his thoughts and feelings straightened out would be a very good thing right about now. Perhaps if he wasn't around to support her as much it would force her to face her own demons. If only answers were as readily available as all the questions.

Smiling ruefully to himself Alex stood up to head to bed. He needed to get some sleep so he was well rested to face getting on a plane tomorrow afternoon. It was a good thing that Sam would be there to support him. Knowing his brother was next to him both relieved and terrified him. Good to have the support but thinking of Sam being on a plane that could crash and kill them both at the same time left him feeling cold.

Stop it Alex, he lectured himself. Think of the statistics of the number of planes that land safely every day compared to the number that actually crash. Think of getting your life back and having a long, happy life. Think of going to bed and getting some rest so you don't sound like a babbling idiot in the meeting tomorrow! Now that's an even better thought!

Sabrina hobbled out to the deck to sit at the table to work on some drawings that were due to a new client soon. Breakfast that morning with Alex was a very quiet somber meal. She hated to think of him flying but knew that this was something that he needed to do. His mom was quiet thinking of her son getting on a plane and worried about that and Alex himself was quiet because of what he was facing. He didn't say anything about any fear he might have but Sabrina knew that he had to be concerned. Not that Alex would ever share that with anybody, since he seemed to prefer dealing with things on his own, but she knew he was feeling stressed.

As the day progressed Sabrina became more frustrated with the drawings she was working on. Every angle and floor plan seemed off to her and she continually erased and redrew but still couldn't come up with a design she was happy with. Unfortunately her thoughts kept going back to Alex and how much she missed him. She got used to him popping out to the deck or in the kitchen, wherever she was working for the day, and offering her a drink, a snack and a smile. She counted on his presence since it always made her feel safe and not having him near made her feel unsettled.

Finally right when Sabrina was heading inside to dinner she heard the phone ring and was relieved to hear Elizabeth yell Alex's name.

"Oh Alex, I'm so glad that you called. How was the flight?"

Not being able to hear Alex's response to that question was both a relief and a worry for Sabrina. His mom was silent for a while listening to Alex so it must have been quite a response to her question.

"I'm so glad honey. Do you want to speak to......" she stopped in mid sentence and listened carefully.

Elizabeth glanced over to see Sabrina near the door. "I understand. She's right......okay honey, I will. I hope the meetings go well. Give my love to Sam" then she hung up.

Elizabeth looked over to Sabrina with a sad smile on her face. "I'm sorry honey. Alex was in a rush to get the rental car and head over to the hotel. He said to tell you he was fine and that he would try to give you a call later."

"That's okay" Sabrina said forcing a smile on her face. "I'm just glad that he arrived safely."

She quietly hobbled over to the dining room chair and sat down. Elizabeth and Betty exchanged worried glances then sat down to join her for dinner.

Later that night as Sabrina was getting ready for bed she thought about Alex and wondered why he hadn't called her. Things seemed okay between them before he left but it was strange to have no contact from him at all. She felt empty not having him there and not being able to talk to him or touch him.

Why wouldn't he call Sabrina worried? It felt like he was trying to distance himself but that didn't make any sense to her. They were getting along pretty well she thought. Other than his frustration with her for not "dealing with things" as he always put it, they were good. Weren't they?

Feeling frustrated with her thoughts Sabrina crawled into bed and laid her head down on her pillow to try and get some sleep. It took several hours of tossing and turning but eventually she fell asleep thinking of Alex.

Sabrina came awake to a loud scream. It took her several minutes before she realized that it was her. Reaching a shaky hand to her temple she felt the sweat pouring off her face. That's right! She was dreaming she remembered. Of Alex and he was hurt and she couldn't get to him. His voice kept calling out to her but she didn't know where he was. There was fire everywhere and the heat was almost too much to bear.

A small light came on in the hallway and the door to Sabrina's room opened up. Betty, wearing a floral robe, peeked in at Sabrina. "I heard a loud noise. Is everything okay?"

Sabrina pushed her hair behind her ear and looked over to Betty. "Everything's fine Betty. Go back to sleep. I'm sorry I disturbed you."

Betty walked all the way in to the room and looked at Sabrina. "You're eyes look funny." She felt her forehead. "Hmm..no fever."

Sabrina pulled her head back from Betty's touch. "Really, I'm fine. Go back to bed. It was just a dream."

"Can I get you something to drink…"

"Really Betty. I'm fine. Thanks anyway."

Betty, looking closely at Sabrina finally nodded her head and headed to the door. "Well, okay but if you need me just call okay?"

"I will. Goodnight."

Sabrina lay in bed for a while reliving the dream she had of Alex. It was disturbing thinking of something happening to him. Even more disturbing was how she felt thinking of him not being around. Knowing he was near was becoming way too important to her peace of mind.

Maybe it was time to head back to her apartment and start her life again Sabrina thought. This attachment to Alex was not a good thing. Being attached to ANYBODY wasn't good. Losing her entire family was a lesson she took to heart and being alone just suited her. This way she wouldn't get hurt when people left, and they almost always left.

Yes, Sabrina thought, better to head home now before this attachment to Alex, his whole family and the feelings she got when she was near them got worse. They weren't her family and she needed to stop pretending that they were. She was strong enough now and could handle getting in and out of her apartment on her own. Kat would be there to help with anything else she needed plus she would be closer to the hospital for her next appointment and the physical therapy people that Doctor Moore wanted her to see.

Yes, that was exactly what she planned on telling Alex as soon as he got back from his business trip. It was best this way, for everybody.

~

THE NEXT TWO DAYS WERE DIFFICULT for Sabrina to get through. She never got back to sleep the first night she had the dream and last night wasn't much better. She tossed and turned and eventually ended up sitting up in bed reading until daylight crept in to her room.

Alex's Mom and Betty kept trying to engage her in conversation but Sabrina preferred to keep to her own counsel. Knowing that they were starting to worry about her she tried to smile and reassure them but her heart just wasn't in it. She was sad to be leaving them and this wonderful house. As necessary as she felt it was, it still hurt.

Later that evening Alex made it home in time to find a lovely dinner ready and waiting for him. When he walked in the door his mom met him with a warm hug.

"Alex, I'm so happy your back. How was the trip?"

"It was good mom. How are things here?"

"Fine."

"Fine? That's it, just fine?"

"Fine is good, isn't it? Not bad, not great."

"Mom...." Alex started.

"Why didn't you call Sabrina? You told me you would, I told her you said you would but you didn't. I think you hurt her feelings Alex. That's not like you."

"I know. Things just got really busy and by the time I had a few moments it was late and I didn't want to wake her. Where is she?"

"That's no excuse Alex" his mother scolded. "She's in the living room working on one of her projects. Go say hi then we'll eat okay?"

Alex nodded to his mother and walked towards the living room. When he got to the door he saw Sabrina looking down at a drawing she had in front of her with a frown on her face. Tossing the pencil down she took the drawing and viscously scrunched it up and tossed it toward the corner waste basket that was overflowing with similar scrunched up pieces of paper. Things must not be going well Alex thought. Afraid to startle her he tapped on the side of the doorway.

Sabrina looked up at the tapping and her heart jumped a little. "You're back."

"I am. From the looks of the garbage over there I'd say you're having a tough time with your drawings."

Sabrina, deciding to be cooler and not appear so needy, simply smirked. "I've had better days. How was your trip?"

"Good. Sorry I didn't call but......".

"No worries" Sabrina interrupted. "You don't owe me anything Alex. I'm sure you and Sam were very busy."

"Sabrina…"

"Is that dinner I smell? I'm sure your Mom has everything all ready. Let's go eat."

Frustrated Alex watched as Sabrina stood up and grabbed her crutches. He went over to see if he could help but she just brushed him away and made her own way in to the dining room. Everything was all on the table and ready so they sat down to dinner. Elizabeth kept a lively flow of conversation, asking Alex about his trip and how the business went. She asked about how he handled the flight to and from and how Sam handled the meetings. Sabrina listened to the sound of Alex's voice knowing that this was the thing that she would miss the most. Just listening to him talk and knowing he was close.

Alex watched Sabrina as dinner progressed worried about the distance she seemed to have put between them. He was frustrated that every time he tried to drawl her into the conversation his efforts were met with short responses and then stony silence. Maybe he was wrong not to call her but he needed some time to think.

After dinner and the dishes were done, the four of them headed in to the living room to watch TV. Forty-five minutes into a movie they were watching, Sabrina stood up and grabbed her crutches.

"I'm heading to bed. Goodnight everybody."

Elizabeth and Betty wished her sweet dreams and continued watching the movie. Alex stood up to go with her but Sabrina stopped him. "I'm fine Alex. I can manage on my own. Enjoy the rest of the movie. I'll see you tomorrow."

Alex watched Sabrina hobble into her bedroom. When she went in Alex turned to his mom. "What was that all about?"

"I don't know honey. She's been pretty quiet since you left."

"She had a pretty bad nightmare that first night you were gone too" Betty interjected. "Last night her light was on most of the night. I think she stayed awake so she wouldn't have another one. I tried giving her something to help her sleep but she refused."

"I'm going to go talk to her then head to bed." Alex kissed his mother's cheek and patted Betty's shoulder. "Goodnight."

~

ALEX KNOCKED ON SABRINA'S DOOR AND waited for her to answer. He waited a few seconds and when none came he tapped again and opened the door. When he peered around the door and looked in she was just coming out from the bathroom with her nightgown on.

"Can we talk" Alex asked.

"I'm really tired Alex, can it wait till tomorrow?"

Alex walked the rest of the way in to her room and sat down on her bed and patted the space beside him. "No actually, it can't."

Eying him suspiciously Sabrina went over to a chair near the bed, sat down and placed her crutches on the floor beside her. Okay, what's up?"

"There" he nearly shouted. "That's what's up. I've been back three hours and you've been distancing yourself from me since then. I'm sorry I didn't call you, I know that wasn't fair. I was really busy and just needed some space to think about a few things."

"Alex, I'm not upset about that. Honestly! I'm not your responsibility and you don't have to answer to me, nor are you required to call me."

"Then why are you so upset? Tell me what I did."

"I'm not upset and you didn't do anything wrong. I've just been thinking too, I have a lot on my mind."

"Like what?"

"Alex, can we just talk about this tomorrow? It's getting late and I…"

"It's 9:00 in the evening Sabrina and we ARE going to talk about this!"

Staring at him, Sabrina knew that he would not let it go. Having this conversation was not what she had planned but better to get it out now and get it over with.

"Well" she began. "I've been thinking a lot about how good your family has been to me. We're heading into colder weather now and your Mom probably wants to get back to your Dad and well….I think it's time I went back to my apartment." Alex just stared at her like she grew a third head so she jumped in again."Kat will be around to help with anything I need and…"

"NO" Alex yelled.

"…I'll be closer to the hospital for my appointments.."

"I SAID NO" Alex shouted jumping up from the bed!

Stunned Sabrina looked over at him. Surely he's joking she thought, until she got a really good look at his face and saw how angry he really was.

Alex paced back and forth like a caged animal for a few minutes then stopped in front of Sabrina's chair. Breathing heavy he just stared at her for a few minutes. After a few deep breaths to calm down he kneeled in front of her to look in her eyes. "Sabrina, you don't need to worry about this right now. Mom is happy staying here for a while and you really should be around people who can take care of you. Betty isn't worried about moving on so there's no reason for you to leave."

Sabrina took a hold of Alex's hand. "I need to go Alex. I have to start getting my life back and this is the first step to doing that.

Alex removed his hand from hers and stood up. "No. You need to stay here for just a little while longer."

"Alex, you're being unreasonable. Besides, I can make my own decisions."

"Evidently you can't because this decision is a bad one. You're not ready yet. Have you thought about what would happen if you fell? Who would be there to hear you, to get help if you needed it? Everything and everyone you need is right here. You're being ridiculous" Alex yelled.

"Me? I think you're overreacting right now. I think…."

"Look, we're both tired" Alex interrupted as he pushed his fingers through his hair in frustration. "Let's just get some sleep and we'll talk about it again in a few days."

"Alex…"

Alex went back to kneeling by Sabrina's chair. He put his hands on her shoulders drawing her forward and placing a soft kiss on her lips. "We'll talk about this later. Get some rest."

With that he stood up then walked over to the door, glanced back at Sabrina and softly closed the door behind him.

This is not over Alex Deluca, Sabrina thought to herself. I can't stay and become more dependent on you. I can't continue to need you like I do. It's just too scary!

~

THE NEXT MORNING ALEX ATE A quick breakfast before Sabrina was even out of bed. He kissed his mom goodbye and headed to his office in Boston to do some work. When Sabrina woke up she wasn't sure if she should be upset that Alex was already gone or happy that she could now follow through with her plan to leave.

The night before she had called Kat to make arrangements for her to drive to the Cape to pick her up and bring her home. Knowing that Alex would pitch a fit she was hoping to make her exit before he got home. The timing seemed to be working out perfectly. Kat would be there before lunch so she should be gone before Alex got back.

After quietly packing as much as she could Sabrina went out to talk to Elizabeth and Betty about leaving. As hard as it was, both Elizabeth and Betty seemed to understand that she needed to go. Sabrina offered to pay Betty for the rest of the month but both women refused saying that Alex had already taken care of Betty's salary for the month.

When Kat arrived to get Sabrina, they all helped to pack her belongings in the car. After everything was in Sabrina turned and gave Betty a warm hug and thanked her for taking such good care of her. Betty's eyes were suspiciously moist as she hugged Sabrina's back and patted her on the shoulder reminding her to call if she ever needed anything.

Sabrina then turned to Elizabeth. "I just don't know how I can possibly thank you for everything you've done for me."

"Ah honey, I wish you didn't feel like you had to go. You know I'd love to have you stay longer."

"I know" Sabrina sniffed. "But I have to. Will you tell Alex I'm sorry? Tell him...tell him I just had to go okay. And tell him that I.....that I care about him and am so grateful for everything he's done for me."

"Why don't you stay and tell him yourself honey."

"I can't. He needed space and I understand that. I'm just asking for the same thing, just some space to figure things out."

"Will you promise to call me if you need anything? Even if it's just a shoulder to lean on" Elizabeth asked with tears in her eyes.

"Oh Mrs. Deluca....I will" Sabrina cried. She put her arms around her and hugged her tightly. "Thank you for being here for me. I love you" she whispered then turned and hopped into the car being careful not to bang her crutches on the window. As Kat started to pull away Sabrina looked over to wave and saw both Betty and Elizabeth waving back to her with tears on their cheeks.

Chapter 14

OCTOBER SOON BECAME NOVEMBER AND STILL Alex's thoughts of Sabrina were never far away. It was hard to believe that it was a month ago when he returned to the Cape after a long day at work only to find that Sabrina had walked, or in her case hobbled away. He still felt hurt and angry that she left without even talking to him. He understood the need for space but what she did and how she did it wasn't necessary. It had taken a lot of willpower not to go to her apartment to see her to make sure she was doing okay but he heard what his mother said about her needing space. So that was what he'd been giving her. He was getting the distinct feeling though that Sabrina wouldn't seek him out. If he wanted to see her he was going to have to be the one to make a move.

Maybe his brother Sam could give him some information on where Sabrina might "happen" to be so he could arrange to bump into her He'd already tried calling her but all he ever got was her answering machine. He never left a message but certainly she could see that he called her several times.

Yes, maybe Sam was his answer. He and Sabrina's assistant Kat have been dating for the past several months so certainly he could tell him what he wanted to know. Maybe even help to arrange a coincidental meeting.

Alex walked out of his office and over to his assistant Mary's desk. Mary looked at Alex with a raised eyebrow. "Can I do something for you Mr. Deluca?"

"Mary, you've worked for me for years now and I continually ask you to call me Alex."

"Yes I have and yes you do Mr. Deluca. Now what can I do for you?"

Smiling Alex shook his head at her. "Nothing. I'm heading to Sam's office for a few. I'll be right back."

"Fine, Sir."

Laughing Alex made his way to the office down the hall from his own. It was actually great that Sam was working with him full time now. Having him around to help carry the burden and to be able to bounce ideas back and forth was working out extremely well. That was one good thing that came out of the whole ordeal of the plane crash, his brother running their company by his side. They made a terrific team, just as Alex has suspected they would.

Abby, Sam's newly hired assistant, was sitting at her desk outside Sam's office.

"Is he in Abby" Alex asked.

"Of course Mr. Deluca. Shall I let him know you need to see him?"

"Don't bother. I'll just go in."

Smiling Alex opened the door to Sam's office to find him sitting behind his desk frowning at his computer. When he heard the door he looked up and frowned harder.

"Did you know that there are some serious issues at Lehman Brothers?"

"I did but I didn't come in here to discuss business" Alex retorted.

Sam looked up in surprise at his brother."Are you ill? Do I need to take you to have a brain scan? Who are you and what have you done with my brother."

"Cut it out Sam. I need a favor."

"I'll do any favor you want if you do one for me."

"If your favor is to let Abby go the answer is no."

Sam just rolled his eyes. "You're no fun Alex. I thought you had my back."

"I do but in this case you're the one who asked Mom to hire an assistant for you. Did you seriously think she would pick some blond bombshell who couldn't think or type to sit right outside your office?"

"No but I did think that she would pick someone......I don't know.... closer to my century in age. Less intimidating.....more...bendable."

Alex laughed out loud. "Bendable? Sam, she's not doing gymnastics, she's your assistant. Besides, Abby is only 62 years old and does her job better than most. She's very good at what she does and you're lucky to have her. Besides, what the hell does bendable mean?"

"She's just very rigid with how she does things. She's really nice and keeps me organized but....I don't know."

"Well Mary speaks very highly of her so I think you should just give it more time. Before you know it you won't be able to live without her. Now, as to my favor; and before you say anything; just hear me out."

"Shoot."

"Well, I know that you've been seeing Kat lately and I was just wondering if maybe you could get an idea from her where Sabrina might be so I could maybe bump into her sometime."

"Seriously Alex? You want me grill Kat about Sabrina's whereabouts so I can report to you where she is so you can....what....stalk her? What are we, back in high school?"

"I know it sounds bad but I'm worried about her and she won't answer my calls."

"Look Alex, I know you're worried but Kat said she was doing fine. Stop worrying. I think she just needs a little more time. I'm sure she'll be in touch with you when she feels she's got a better handle on things."

Sighing Alex walked to the door and turned back to face Sam. "You're right. Sorry I asked. I just.....miss her."

As he started to close the door Sam called out "I heard something about her being at the hospital this afternoon, right after lunch."

Alex popped his head back in the door. "Why? Is something wrong with her?"

"No, at least I don't think so. Could be just a checkup. I don't really know. I just heard Kat mention she would be there."

"Thanks Sam. I appreciate it."

Alex spent the rest of the morning trying to concentrate on work but his thoughts kept going back to Sabrina. Seriously, how could he just bump into Sabrina at the hospital without looking like he was waiting around just to see her? How pathetic was that. What possible excuse could he say on why he was even there? Sabrina would see right through that. Although, he was a board member at the hospital so he could always say he was there on hospital business. Yeah, like a board member would be walking around, lurking in hospital hallways. Not likely!

Shelving the idea for the time being he returned to the work at hand and finished the analysis that was due to be faxed over to a client. Finally around noon he decided to go out for a bite of lunch and some fresh air.

After wolfing down a sausage from one of the local venders he started walking and before he knew it he was near the hospital. Not really thinking, he continued the rest of the way and walked in to the lobby area. He stood for a few minutes and deciding that he felt ridiculous for being there he turned to go back out. Out of the corner of his eye he saw a flash of pink and when he turned, there was Sabrina walking onto the elevator.

Surprised, he stood there and watched as she entered the elevator alone and the doors closed. Not sure where she was going he watched the elevator lights to see that it stopped at the seventh floor. Although he realized that it could have stopped to let passengers on and not necessarily to let her off, Alex decided to take a chance anyway and headed to the seventh floor.

Alex entered the elevator along with several other passengers who materialized out of nowhere. After stopping at just about every floor between the ground floor and the seventh floor to let people off, the elevator doors finally opened up to let him off at the seventh floor.

As he walked off the elevator and down the hall he passed a window on his left. When he looked in he realized that this was the maternity floor. Thinking that she couldn't possibly have gotten off on this particular floor, Alex started to turn around when he caught that same flash of pink again. When he stopped and looked to his right he saw Sabrina sitting in a rocking chair and watched as a nurse gently placed a tiny baby with tubes sticking out everywhere into her waiting arms. Farther down from Sabrina there were several other rocking chairs with other women holding tiny infants and rocking back and forth.

His gaze wondered back to Sabrina as she took the child into her arms and nuzzled the baby's cheek with her nose. She began gently rocking back and forth. Alex could see that her lips were moving so she was either talking to the baby or singing a lullaby.

The nurse that had placed the baby in Sabrina's arms walked out so Alex stopped her. "Excuse me, can I ask you a question?"

"Sure. What can I do for you?"

"Those women in there, holding the babies, are any of them the mothers?"

"Why do you ask?" The nurse looked Alex up and down with suspicion in her eyes.

Realizing that the nurse probably thought he was asking to cause trouble he smiled down at her. "My name is Alex Deluca. I'm one of the board members here at the hospital. Sabrina is a friend of mine and I just saw her in there and was curious."

Smiling the nurse looked back in to the room where Sabrina was sitting. "Those are a few of the volunteers that Sabrina has organized to come in to hold these particular babies."

"Why these particular babies" Alex asked.

"Because their mothers are either not here or are not well enough to care for their children."

The nurse continued to explain to Alex how the babies in this particular unit were born from mothers who had an addiction of some kind, whether it was from alcohol or drugs. Since the mothers were unable to care for their child, or in some cases the child was a ward of the state, these volunteers were stepping in to do what the nurses caring for them couldn't. Take time to hold and rock them, to have the infant feel the warmness of another human touch.

She continued to explain how it was difficult to organize volunteers because there were times when there weren't any infants in need so no volunteers were needed. Other times, like now, there were several that needed attention.

"So how long has this group of volunteers been around?"

"Only for about three weeks. As I said, it's tough finding volunteers. Once you find anyone interested, there are background checks that have to be done before they're allowed anywhere near this unit. Sabrina's worked really hard getting this in place."

"Sabrina?"

"Didn't she tell you? This is "her baby" so to speak. She approached the board, got the approval and has been getting the volunteers, the background checks completed and working on the scheduling. It's been kind of hard because she has more volunteers but they haven't been approved yet so she can't use them. For now these three are it. Since you're a board member, didn't you hear about this when she presented it?"

"I haven't been able to attend the last few board meetings" Alex mumbled. "My brother stepped in to cover my place with the board for a while and he didn't mention anything. Thanks for talking to me, I guess I better get back to work."

The nurse nodded her head at Alex and started toward the other nursery to continue her rounds. Alex watched Sabrina for a few more minutes then headed back to the elevators to go back to work.

Once back at his office he sat at his desk thinking about what Sabrina had accomplished. He was so proud of her and what she was doing. He remembered that she had visited that nursery at the hospital they were in after the plane crash. That was probably where she got the idea he realized.

Could this be how she was healing herself he wondered? Maybe she didn't need to see a therapist or psychologist like everybody, including him, was trying to force her to do. After all, everybody was different and not everybody dealt with things the same way. Maybe she needed to handle things in her own way. This, as Alex thought about, was exactly what Sabrina herself had said to him.

I'm an idiot, Alex thought! Maybe it was time to listen to what Sabrina wanted and thought instead of being so sure that he had all the answers. Whether it was in regards to her recovery or thoughts on their relationship. Remembering his dictate that she was to stay at the Cape when she felt she was ready to leave probably was not the smartest move he had ever made and probably was why she ran and has been avoiding him ever since.

Deciding that it was time to have a face to face chat, Alex dug into the pile of work that needed to be completed by the end of the day. He had every intention of leaving the office on time this evening. He had plans to meet Ms Wallace at her apartment where she couldn't brush him off so easily!

SABRINA SHIFTED HER BRIEFCASE STRAP UP her left shoulder again and moved the small bag of groceries from her right hand to her left. She grabbed on to the rail to the steps leading up to her apartment and stopped short when a voice asked if he could help.

She knew that voice! It was the one she had been avoiding for a while. Now he was here, right on her front stoop and there was no where she could go to avoid him now. It was one thing to be reasonable about her feelings when he wasn't near her but having him here was not good! Seeing him, hearing him, even smelling him did things to her equilibrium! It did things to her like making her want to push aside all those sharply honed decisions that she was better off being alone. Then he comes along making her question that decision.

Alex reached down from the top step and grabbed her grocery bag. "Should you be carrying this much weight with your legs still recovering?"

"Well, hello to you too Alex" Sabrina grumbled.

Rolling his eyes Alex sighed. "Sorry. Hello Sabrina."

"What brings you to my front stoop Alex?"

"I'd like to talk to you if that's okay."

"Look Alex, I'm pretty busy......" she began.

"Please Sabrina. I've been trying to get in touch with you for a while and you've been avoiding me."

Hesitating, Sabrina looked up and into Alex's eyes. She shouldn't let him in but she felt so drawn to him. She missed their conversations and his gentle caresses. Would it really be so bad to let him in just for a few minutes?

Deciding that it would be fine and that she really did want to see him, even for a short time, she just nodded her head and continued up the steps. Alex followed her in and up to her apartment. When they entered he looked for the kitchen and finding it on his left he walked in that direction to place her grocery bag on the counter. Sabrina put her briefcase down and joined him in the kitchen.

"Do want anything to drink" she asked.

"No, I'm fine. You look good Sabrina. How are you feeling?"

"I'm good, still going to physical therapy. I won't be running any marathons anytime soon but things are progressing well. How are you doing?"

"I'm good. I've missed you."

Sabrina looked away, not wanting to see what was in his eyes. Or for him to see what was in her eyes. She missed him, way too much!

"I saw you today Sabrina" Alex continued.

She looked up at him with a start. "Where? I didn't see you."

"You were busy. In fact you had a tiny baby in your arms."

"You were at the hospital? Why?"

Now that was a question he walked right in to without thinking, and didn't know how to answer without sounding pathetic. He decided to try to gloss over the reasons and simply said "I had some business there." Hoping to distract her he continued on quickly, "One of the nurses there mentioned that you started a volunteer group to help those babies."

"I did."

Alex took a hold of Sabrina's hand and gently rubbed across her knuckles. "I think what you're doing is admirable. I'm really proud of you Brie."

"Thanks Alex."

For the next ten minutes or so they chatted back and forth catching each other up on their lives. They both started laughing when Alex brought up the fact that Sam and Kat had been dating. They seemed like such an odd couple but strangely enough, they both seemed pretty smitten with the other.

Smiling Sabrina said, "I never thought I would see Kat so taken with a guy. It's really quite nice to see."

"I know. Sam was always flitting from one woman to the next but he seems genuinely happy. More settled than I've ever seen him. Poor Mom doesn't know what to make of him."

They both started to laugh but when the laughter died down there was an awkward silence.

"I meant what I said outside Brie. I really miss you."

"Alex, I don't think…."

Alex took a hold of Sabrina's shoulders and gently pulled her closer.

"Alex……….."

Looking into his eyes it was hard for Sabrina to pull away. They just stared at each other for a few seconds then Alex brought her against his chest. Slowly he leaned in and kissed her very lightly on the lips. Pulling back slightly he looked at her to gage her reaction. Seeing that she was not backing away, he brought his hands up and cupped her head. Slanting his head he brought his lips crushing down onto hers in a carnal need that overwhelmed them both. His tongue touched her bottom lip, rubbing softly as if asking for permission to enter. Sighing she opened her lips and their tongues dueled back and forth.

Releasing her face, Alex put his arms around her and pulled her tighter against his body. Sabrina put her arms up and around Alex's shoulders, her fingers playing with the hair on the back of his collar. She too pulled on Alex's body drawing him even closer, feeling his obvious erection between them. Reveling in the knowledge that he obviously felt as attracted to her as she was to him, she sighed and deepened the kiss.

A phone ringing somewhere in the distance brought Sabrina to her senses. Pulling back she looked at Alex and said in a soft voice "I better get that."

Smiling Alex let her go. "If you must."

Sabrina walked over to her purse on shaky legs, took out her cell phone and answered the call.

Alex listened for a few seconds, long enough to get that it was one of her clients calling, then walked away to give her some privacy. While she was talking and writing some notes Alex took the opportunity to walk around her apartment. Her living room, much like the dining room, was neatly kept with basic yet elegant furnishings. There was a Bose sound system in one corner of the room so he wondered over to look at the CD's she had collected. As he perused through them he saw that she had an eclectic taste, varying from classical to rock. She had several Dave Matthew CD's as well as a few Led Zeppelin. In the middle of the room against the wall and situated between two windows she had a large screen plasma TV with a DVD left open on the side. He walked over to see that she had left out *The Towering Inferno* so she must have watched it recently. When he kneeled down to look at the rest of her collection he saw movies like *The Birds,* an old Alfred Hitchcock movie, several Steven King movies and a lot of romance looking titles that he didn't recognize.

He sat down on the couch facing the TV and propped his ankle over his knee with his hand on the back of her sofa. Listening to her finishing up the conversation he looked over and waited for her to come into the living room. When she appeared next to him he reached for her hand.

Sabrina carefully moved her arm to the side so he couldn't reach her hand then looked down at him.

"Look Alex, I have things I need to do tonight."

Alex stood up and frowned at her. "I think we have a lot more to say to each other, don't you."

"Alex….don't take this the wrong way but I have a lot to do. Besides, there really isn't much more to say. You yourself indicated that we needed to get on with our lives and I have. I don't need any complications right now. I'm just starting to get my life back together."

"And what was that kiss? It didn't mean anything to you? Because I won't believe you if you say that. I know you felt what I did. We have chemistry Brie and I think we should explore where that might lead us. It could be something really good."

"Look Alex, I like being with you but this just can't lead to anything. I just don't want a relationship."

"With me" he asked.

"With anybody Alex. Believe me, I'm better off alone."

Alex pushed his hand through his hair in frustration. "You can't mean that Sabrina. That's ridiculous. Everybody needs to have someone in their life. Is it because of the crash? Your parents" Alex asked trying to understand.

Alex was getting way too close to the truth so Sabrina began to panic. She had absolutely no intention of laying open her soul for him to analyze. Especially knowing that she would come up lacking in the process.

"That's not it Alex" she said raising her voice. "You have no idea what I've been through or even who I am. Don't you get it, I'm just not interested."

Alex couldn't believe what she just said. "So you won't even give us a chance? You really think it's better to be alone the rest of your life? Are you so afraid that someone will leave you that you're not even willing to take a chance? How warm does that keep you at night Sabrina?"

Sabrina turned away from Alex and walked over to her door and opened it, looking back expectantly at him.

Alex walked over to the door and stopped by her side. Speaking softly he said, "You know Sabrina, some day you're going to look back at your life and realize that you made a huge mistake. I just hope that when that day comes, I just might still be around." He kissed her forehead and walked out the door.

Sabrina quietly shut the door and walked into her bedroom. She went over to her bed, lay down with her face in her pillow and started sobbing.

LATER THAT WEEK SABRINA WAS WORKING in her home office when she heard her doorbell ring. Fearing it might be Alex she ignored the buzzer and continued to work. Eventually the noise ended and she was able to concentrate on her project. She had just gotten focused on her work again when her cell phone rang. Feeling frustrated with the interruption she glanced at her phone saw that it was Kat and answered it with relief.

"Hi Kat."

"I'm coming over for lunch. Do you have anything there or should I pick something up on the way there" she asked.

"What's wrong" Sabrina asked.

"Nothing, we haven't seen each other in a while since you've decided to work at home and not at the office. You've been pushing me off and only communicating through calls and e-mails so I wanted to get together. So what'll it be?"

Hesitating, Sabrina thought about what was in her fridge. "Since you're not giving me a choice you better stop on the way. I haven't been shopping for a few days. Just grab me whatever you're having."

"Great. See you in about twenty minutes. Open the door for me this time. You ignored me a few minutes ago." With that Kat hung up leaving Sabrina to wonder what bug was up her friends butt! From the tone of her voice, this was not going to be good.

At exactly twenty minutes later the doorbell rang again and Sabrina stopped working to buzz Kat in. Opening her front door she walked out to the landing to yell down and see if Kat needed any help carrying things in.

Declining any assistance Kat made her way up and into the apartment. After she put her bag down on the kitchen table she took her coat off, threw it across a chair in the dining room and turned to look at Sabrina.

"Well" she harrumphed looking her up and down. "You look like shit."

"Wow Kat. You sure know how to make a girl feel good about herself."

"Well now, that wasn't really why I came here. What's going on? I'd guess you've lost about 10 pounds, which you couldn't afford to lose by the way, and you must not be sleeping because those dark circles under your eyes tell me the truth."

"I'm fine. Just a little stressed working on two different projects at the same time and trying to meet the deadlines. Stop mothering me."

Shaking her head Katherine moved to the table and began setting out their lunch. She walked over to the fridge to get something to drink and was surprised when she opened it to see that it consisted of some mustard, butter and a few old grapes rolling around the bottom drawer. "Really Brie? Everything is fine? Look at this fridge. You have nothing in here to eat. What are you living on?"

"Pop tarts, okay. Honestly Kat, leave it alone."

"Well, you and Alex both must be suffering from the same affliction. Being around either of you is like sparring with a porcupine and you both look like crap. What gives?"

"Leave it alone, okay Kat. I don't feel like talking about it."

"Okay, fine don't talk about it. But I need you to listen to me for two minutes. I don't understand why you're pushing Alex away. You're both miserable and unhappy, which makes Sam and me miserable and unhappy. You need to get your head on straight. There's no shame in needing or loving someone. For years now I've watched as you cocooned yourself up in this damnable apartment pushing anybody away that just might get close to you. You need to stop it Brie. Your parents wouldn't want you living like this. Hell, I don't want you living like this. I know how you felt when your parents died, I was there, and I saw you. But it's time to join the living. Stop existing for work. Start having some fun and let people in that shell you've formed."

With that Kat stood up and grabbed her coat and put it on. Turning back to Sabrina she glared at her and said, "I'm going back to the office. I'll leave my lunch. You need it more than I do."

And with that she marched out the door and slammed it in her wake.

Sabrina just looked at the food that was on the table, wrapped it all up, not even bothering to eat her own lunch, and stuck it in the fridge. Sighing heavily she went back to her drawing board.

Chapter 15

SABRINA SPENT THE DAYS LEADING UP to the holidays working, taking on as many clients as she possibly could. She started going back to her office instead of working from home, which to her way of thinking, was a step in the right direction. She and Kat settled into a quiet truce, neither bringing up the verbal battle that had taken place in her apartment.

She spent Thanksgiving having a quiet dinner in her apartment alone and wondering what Alex was doing. She could almost imagine his entire family around a dining room table laughing and having a good time. Kat had tried to get her to join them but she just couldn't make herself go. To see Alex would just make her want to get closer to him. According to Kat he wasn't seeing anybody but that could have changed in the two weeks since she asked Kat about him. It hurt to think that he might find someone else, but he was a wonderful man and deserved to find someone that would make him happy. Someone that wasn't afraid to let him get close or who was afraid to commit.

Geez, Sabrina thought to herself. I'm so completely screwed up. It would be so wonderful to be more like Kat who was fun loving and carefree. She was almost jealous of the relationship she and Sam shared.

They seemed so perfect for each other. Their relationship seemed to be moving forward in leaps and bounds. Sometimes it was hard to hear Kat talk about Sam because invariably, Alex's name would come up. At times Sabrina just hung on hoping to get some small detail of how he was, and at other times it just hurt to hear anything about him!

The days leading up to Christmas were hardest of all. Sabrina spent a lot of time working and avoiding any conversations with Kat. Some evenings she walked along the streets looking in the store windows at the displays and enjoying the Christmas lights. Some evenings she just went back to her apartment and sat in front of her little tree remembering when her parents were alive and how much they enjoyed this holiday. Sometimes the memories helped her; sometimes they just made her feel more alone.

When Sabrina wasn't working to meet deadlines for her clients she spent time at the hospital. Her volunteer group, which she named *Loving Hands,* was going strong. She was up to twelve volunteers and she was proud that there wasn't a day that went by where one of the volunteers wasn't in the hospital. Except, of course, when there wasn't a child in need of love and attention, which made those days the way they should be!

At the end of January Sabrina was contacted by the hospital where her volunteer group worked, and asked if she would be willing to take on a new project for her architecture firm. After seeing all the good that *Loving Hands* was doing, the hospital administration wanted to have several rooms remodeled to accommodate the volunteers and the children in need. Sabrina was so excited to take on the project that she assured them that she could come up with several designs for them to look at.

She worked tirelessly for three weeks leading up to her presentation. Several times she spoke to the nurses to get ideas from them on certain things that they felt would benefit the unit. After all, who better to speak to than the nurses that were intimately involved with the care of these special children! If anybody needed ways to make their jobs easier it was these angels who spent their lives doing for others.

The day of the presentation Sabrina dressed with meticulous care. It was important to her to show them that she was professional and in control. This project was near and dear to her heart and she wanted it to go smoothly. Dressing in a navy pencil cut skirt with a white blouse and matching jacket, she added a splash of color by adding one of her mother's favorite fuchsia flowered pins to the lapel. Putting on her navy pumps with low heels, she grabbed her briefcase and left her apartment feeling confident.

She arrived at the hospital in plenty of time to meet Kat and set up the projector for her presentation. Confirming that everything was set and ready to go she stood confidently in the front of the room and waited for the three gentlemen from the hospital administration team to arrive.

The door opened and the gentleman that had contacted her about the project, Bob Anderson, walked in to the room followed by the other two men that were there to help evaluate her work and make the decision. She smiled and approached to shake their hands. After being introduced to the other two men, the door to the boardroom opened again and in walked three more men and two ladies. Sabrina was more than surprised that more people were attending but particularly shocked when she saw that Alex was one of the other men.

"Sabrina" Bob started."I would like to introduce you to the members of the hospital board. Since they're the ones that have approved going forward with this project and have allocated the funds, we felt it was important that they attend so they could provide some feedback. I hope that's okay with you."

Sabrina smiled and reached out to shake the board members hands. "Of course it is."

She was introduced to the first two men and the women who promptly walked over to take a seat at the table. Alex hung back and was the last to be introduced. When Bob started to introduce him Alex mentioned that he and Sabrina already knew each other. Bob smiled then asked if Sabrina could be ready to start in ten minutes. She shook her head yes and Bob walked away to speak to the other board members.

Alex looked down at Sabrina with a raised eyebrow. "I'm sorry if this makes you uncomfortable. I didn't know that you were the architect they hired. I should have guessed it though."

"No worries. It's fine. I didn't know the board would be attending until you all walked in."

"Would you feel better if I excused myself?"

Sabrina sighed. "Of course not. We're professionals Alex. It's not a big deal."

Alex looked at Sabrina for a few long seconds then shook his head and went to take a seat at the opposite end of the table to where she would be standing for her presentation. Great she thought, that put him in her direct line of vision.

Shaking her head, Sabrina walked over to take her position at the front of the room to wait for Bob to get the meeting going. Please she thought to herself; let me get through this without making a fool of myself!

Bob called the meeting to order then promptly handed it over to Sabrina to start. At first she was a little hesitant, knowing that Alex was watching her. After the first few slides though, her passion for this particular project took over and she settled into a rhythm and her presentation flowed.

ALEX WATCHED SABRINA AS SHE WALKED to the front of the room. She looked beautiful. She'd obviously lost more weight than Kat had indicated but she was still stunning. He'd spent the holidays trying not to think of her alone but this was what she'd chosen. It took everything he had not to go to her apartment and try to force her to come with him to spend the holidays with his family. She made it clear; however, that she didn't want him. As much as it hurt and worried him, he had to respect her decision.

He watched her as the presentation continued. It was obvious that she was nervous but as she got further into it, her confidence grew and he loved watching her in her element. It was obvious that she was passionate about this project and he was so damn proud of her right now. Looking around the board room, he could see that she had them all eating out of the palm of her hand. She was good, he thought. It was such a shame that this confidence didn't roll over to her personal life.

~

SABRINA WRAPPED UP HER PRESENTATION AND opened the floor for any questions. After fielding several, Bob stood up to thank Sabrina for her efforts, telling her that they would be back in touch with her with the next few weeks with a decision. Before everybody was dismissed he thanked Alex for his contribution that allowed this project to move forward saying that without Deluca Enterprises, they would not be able complete the remodel.

Alex just smiled and said something about it being a cause he also believed in and stood as the other board members rose to leave. Each one stopped to shake Sabrina's hand and to thank her before leaving.

Once again Alex hung back until everyone left and approached Sabrina as the door closed leaving them alone.

"I didn't know that you were the financial backer that Bob mentioned when he asked me about being the architect."

"My donations are not something I really advertise."

"So why this project Alex?"

Alex hesitated briefly before saying "While I didn't know that you were the architect, I knew that it was for your volunteer organization and I wanted to help."

Sabrina stepped closer to Alex and put her hand on his sleeve. "Thank you" she whispered.

'You're welcome." Alex hesitated briefly before saying "Look Sabrina, I know how you feel and where we stand. I just.....I have a few questions about this project and thought maybe we could have dinner together to talk about a few things. As colleagues, nothing else."

"I don't think that's a good idea......"

"Just dinner, nothing else. Please?"

Sabrina hesitated briefly then nodded her head in agreement. "Just dinner Alex, nothing else."

"I'll pick you up at your place at 6:00. How's that?"

Shaking her head she just responded with "Fine".

"I have to get to another meeting." Touching her arm he squeezed gently. "I'll see you at 6:00 then." With that he was out the door.

Sabrina sagged into one of closest chairs and let out a long breath. Kat came rushing into the room. "I just saw Alex in the hallway, why was he here? What did he want? Oh…and how did the presentation go?"

"You couldn't have come back in when the presentation ended? I was left alone with Alex. Did you know he was going to be here?"

Kat looked offended. "You really think I would set you up like that? Seriously?"

Sabrina shook her head. "I'm sorry Kat. Alex was here because not only is he a board member of the hospital, but evidently he's the financial backer for the remodel. And the presentation went very well. I think they'll buy into the designs."

"That's really great Brie. I'm happy for you. I know how important this is to you. So what happened with Alex? Did he say anything?"

"Not really. He has a few additional questions so he asked me to go to dinner with him so we could discuss them."

Kat perked up at that news and Sabrina shook her head. "Don't get excited Kat, it's dinner…between two colleagues working on a project together, nothing more."

"If you say so."

~

LATER THAT NIGHT SABRINA STOOD STARING at her closet, trying to figure out what to wear. Jeans seemed too casual but a dress would make it look like she was out on a date as opposed to a dinner between colleagues. Maybe agreeing to go out to dinner was a big mistake she thought. Any discussions about the project should be done in an office, not over a candlelit dinner. What a weak, weak woman to have agreed to this. One look into his beautiful brown eyes and she didn't have a shot in hell of saying no. Stupid!!

After discarding one outfit after another she finally decided on a pair of khaki slacks with a white blouse with a chocolate brown sweater over top. A long gold chain added just the right amount of bling. Added with a flat brown pair of loafers and she was ready to go.

Oh why didn't I just tell him I would meet him at a restaurant she thought? That would have been the smart thing to do. But then when she was around Alex, smart wasn't an adjective that applied! Too late now anyway she realized as the buzzer sounded letting her know that he was here to pick her up.

She grabbed her coat and locked her apartment door then headed downstairs. When she opened the door Alex was surprised to see that she was ready to go.

"I would have come upstairs to get you" he murmured.

"That's okay, I was ready."

Frowning Alex led her down the front steps of her apartment building and with his hand at the small of her back, guided her to his car parked half a block away. When he settled her into the passenger seat he went around getting behind the steering wheel.

When Sabrina was seated she buckled her seatbelt and took a deep breath through her nose. The car smelled like Alex, leather and a subtle hint of aftershave.

As he pulled out into traffic, Alex reached over and turned some music on. After listening for a few minutes Sabrina looked over at him. "So where are we going?"

Alex glanced over at her with a smile on his face. "Just a quiet place that I know that has wonderful food and a quiet atmosphere. Do you like Italian?"

"That's perfect. I love Italian."

Alex drove about ten more minutes then pulled up in to an apartment complex, pulling under the awning. A doorman came out and opened the passenger side door. Looking over at Alex Sabrina asked "Where are we?"

Alex got out of his car and came over to Sabrina's side of the car. By then the doorman had helped her out. Alex took a hold of her hand and guided her through the front door. "My place."

Sabrina pulled her hand out of his and shook her head. "I thought we were having dinner."

"We are! I made my special homemade spaghetti sauce, which is out of this world by the way, and garlic bread." Bowing slightly with a boyish grin on his face and his hand charmingly stretched to the elevator he looked to Sabrina. "Shall we?"

"You're a frustrating man Alex. I thought we were going to a restaurant to eat"

"Why? I asked if we could have dinner together. I didn't say specifically where. You assumed that part. Besides, what's the big deal? We're just two colleagues getting together to discuss a project."

The elevator pinged and the doors opened. Sabrina looked warily at Alex then got in the elevator. Alex entered after her and hit the button for the twelfth floor. When they reached his floor he guided Sabrina to his apartment and unlocked the door. When they entered Alex helped her off with her coat and hung both of them on the rack near the entrance. He moved further into the apartment and turned to Sabrina.

"Come in. Make yourself at home."

Sabrina closed her eyes and inhaled. The smell of spaghetti sauce lingered in the air and made her stomach growl appreciatively. When she opened her eyes Alex was staring at her, a smile lifting the corners of his mouth.

"I heard that from over here. Hungry?"

"Actually, I am."

Alex was frowning when he said, "You've lost weight Brie.You're not taking very good care of yourself."

"I'm fine, just busy. Besides, I didn't come here for a lecture."

Holding his hands up in a gesture of compliance he moved further into the apartment toward the kitchen. Sabrina followed him in and was mesmerized when she rounded the corner and saw the view of Boston from his windows. Slowly she looked around his apartment taking in the beautiful open floor plan that encompassed the kitchen with a breakfast bar, his dining room and the living room that boasted of a soft leather sectional facing a plasma TV, a fireplace and a stunning view of the city lights.

Alex watched her face as she looked around his apartment. It was stupid but he was anxious to see what she thought of where he lived. It never bothered him before what a woman thought of his place, but this particular woman and her thoughts mattered to him.

"What a stunning home you have Alex. It's so elegant but just invites you to come in and get comfortable."

Alex walked over to the stove to stir his sauce. "I have everything ready; I just need to bake the garlic bread. Why don't you take a look around while I finish this up."

Sabrina nodded and walked over to the windows to look out at the view. She looked around for a few moments then moved down the hall a bit, looking at the pictures on his walls in the hallway leading to the back of his apartment. She smiled when she saw pictures of his parents, both at the Cape and what must be there home here. They were several of him and Sam when they were younger and few that were more recent. There were a couple of Alex with a group of people on what must have been a tour of some kind. Looking closer Sabrina saw that Alex had his arm around one woman and they looked very happy. Jealousy pierced her heart, even though she knew she had no right to feel that way.

Moving on down the hallway she looked into the first room on her right which was obviously his home office. Further down there was a spare bedroom and on the right and a bathroom on the left. The last door that was directly in front of her was Alex's bedroom. Not being able to stop herself she stepped in and looked around. This room just felt like Alex. The furniture was a dark mahogany wood. He had another beautiful view of the city skyline with a walk-in closet that he had left open, a master bathroom and a fireplace with two chairs sitting in front of it. The comforter on his king sized bed was hunter green with thin cream stripes and accent pillows in the center.

Sabrina closed her eyes imagining Alex sleeping in that bed. His scent was hanging softly in the air making her skin tingle. She opened her eyes and saw Alex standing by the doorway watching her.

Embarrassed she smiled and said "This is a really nice place Alex." She brushed passed him heading back out to the living room. Alex followed her out to the kitchen and offered her a glass of wine. She sat at the breakfast bar, sipping her wine and keeping him company as he finished making their dinner.

"Can I help with anything?"

Alex was taking a bowl of salad from the refrigerator. "Nope, almost set. Just a few more minutes for the bread and we can eat."

"So do you do a lot of cooking? It smells heavenly."

"To be honest spaghetti is the one dish I do well. I can cook other stuff but nothing gourmet. I usually keep it pretty simple."

After a few seconds of silence Sabrina decided to dive right in. "So Alex, what were those questions you wanted to ask me?"

"Why don't we sit down to eat and we'll talk then okay?"

Sabrina nodded and watched as Alex took the garlic bread from the oven. He drained the spaghetti and placed servings on each plate and placed the sauce on top. Refilling both of their wine glasses they sat down and started eating. After making sure that Sabrina liked the dinner, Alex brought up the questions that he wanted to ask about the project. Sabrina answered each one with clear concise responses, impressing Alex with her business sense.

By the time they had finished their dinner and a third glass of wine, Sabrina sat back in her seat smiling.

"So what's that smile about" Alex asked.

"Well, to be honest, I thought you didn't really have any questions and that this was just a ploy to get me to have dinner with you."

Not wanting to admit that that was indeed the truth and that he had spent the afternoon racking his brain for some intelligent questions to ask, he just smiled and said "I'm wounded Sabrina."

"I bet."

Standing Alex grabbed their plates and headed in to the kitchen. Sabrina followed with the rest of the dishes from the table and helped stack them in the dishwasher. Alex poured them each a cup of coffee and suggested they head in to the living room to relax with their coffee. He offered dessert but Sabrina declined, having eaten too much of the spaghetti.

They chatted for a while about their work, Kat and Sam and how well they were doing and Alex's parents. During one of the brief pauses Sabrina put her coffee cup down and stood up.

"I really should be going Alex. I can grab a cab instead of you going out in the cold to drive me home."

Alex stood up and grabbed her elbow. "Please, stay a while longer."

"I shouldn't. We both have work tomorrow and I just think that my being here longer would just complicate things."

"What are you afraid of Brie?" Alex stepped closer to Sabrina looking down into her eyes. "Why won't you let me in?"

Closing her eyes she sighed heavily. "We've been through this before. I just can't Alex. Please, try and understand."

"That's just it Brie. I don't understand. You're excluding everyone from your life. Even Kat said you were distancing yourself from her, and she was the one person you used to allow around you. It's obvious that you're not eating or sleeping and people are worried about you. Hell, I'm worried about you!"

"Let it go Alex."

Alex looked down into her eyes and bringing his hand up he cupped her cheek. "I can't. I care about you" he whispered.

Alex leaned his head down and rested his forehead against Sabrina's for a brief minute. "I need to know that you're okay."

"Oh Alex" Sabrina sighed right before he cupped her other cheek, looked into her eyes and leaned in to kiss her.

After a few moments of hesitation Sabrina surrendered her self control and placed her arms around Alex's neck and pulled him in as close as she could to deepen the kiss. Their tongues met and tangled with each other until they both pulled away breathless.

They stared at each other breathing heavily waiting to see what the other one would do. Taking the initiative Alex slowly took the lapels of her sweater and pushed it off her shoulders and peeled it off her arms. Dropping it on the floor behind her, he leaned in again to capture her lips with his. At the same time he began unbuttoning her blouse. One button after the other popped open until he stepped back slightly to pull the blouse from her slacks. Sabrina looked down, having just now realized what he had done. When she started to pull away he brought her against him.

"Don't" he whispered.

After a short battle with her conscious, Sabrina slowly lifted her arms and started unbuttoning Alex's shirt. She may regret this later but right now, right this moment, she needed him desperately. She needed to feel his arms around her and she needed to know what it felt like to be his, even if it was just for now.

Pulling his shirt from his pants, Sabrina lovingly touched his chest, feeling the contours that defined his abs. She kissed and licked his nipples, hearing him groan in pleasure.

Impatiently Alex pulled her blouse off and threw it aside. Seeing her standing there in her pink lacy bra just did it for him. His hands gently cupped both her breasts and squeezed.

Reaching behind her he unclasped her bra and gently pulled the straps down her arms. Standing there with nothing on top Sabrina made a move to cover her breasts with her hands. Alex pulled them down to her sides so he could look his fill. "My God you're beautiful."

He leaned down and took one pert nipple into his mouth. Sabrina felt a tug all the way down past her stomach. What this man could do to her with a simple touch! She watched as he licked and sucked first one nipple then the other. What a sight to see…this beautiful, strong man feasting on her.

As Alex continued to worship at her breasts, he reached down and unsnapped her slacks and undid her zipper. Releasing her nipple from his mouth he leaned down and gently pushed her slacks and underwear down past her hips, past her thighs and over her calves. He kneeled at her feet and removed her shoes and socks then pulled the rest of her clothing off, tossing them on the floor with the rest of her clothing.

Standing to his full height, Alex stepped back to look at Sabrina. "I've wanted this moment for a long time. You're everything I dreamed and more." He stepped closer for another kiss, gliding his hands over her body to feel the lines and curves he found so tempting.

Breathless Sabrina gently shoved him back. "One of us is overdressed and I don't think it's me."

Chuckling Alex hurriedly removed his clothing. After adding them to the pile he stood before Sabrina in all his naked glory.

"Oh my" she whispered.

"I hope that oh my means I haven't disappointed you."

Sabrina looked him up and down. From his rock hard abs to his muscular thighs and calves, what complaint could she possibly have? There wasn't an inch of spare flesh anywhere on his body. When her eyes drifted to his groin, his erection was hard and jutting out begging for attention. He was certainly blessed with more than average equipment she thought. Not that she had all that much experience to compare him with but...wow!

Stepping towards him Sabrina went down on her knees. Looking up at him for permission, Alex nodded slightly then took in a deep breath. When he felt Sabrina's lips gently touch the crown he sucked in even more. Jesus that felt good. Leaning forward he pushed the tip of his penis into her mouth. As her warm wet mouth took him in Alex felt like he had died and gone to heaven.

After a few tentative strokes she started a rhythm that had him almost coming before he wanted to. Grabbing her by the shoulders he lifted her off her knees and into his embrace.

"If you keep doing that baby I won't last."

After kissing her deeply he picked her up in his arms and headed back to his bedroom. He set her down on her feet long enough to pull the comforter back. He picked her up and gently laid her in the middle of the bed. He followed her down and gently spread her legs. "My turn" he whispered.

Sabrina was floating between reality and the dream that was Alex. It felt so good to have his tongue circling her clit. He seemed to know what would feel good to her and just what spots to hit that took her to the edge. Just when she thought she was about to come he would pull back, bring her back from the edge only to push her back up the hill again.

Finally, after the third frustrating climb he stopped. Thinking he was leaving her hanging again she started to shift her hips back and forth. "Easy baby. I'm right here with you."

Alex came up over Sabrina and slowly started to enter her. "Sweet Jesus you're tight. We'll take this slow baby. I don't want to hurt you."

"Please" Sabrina begged. "Just finish it."

Chuckling Alex kissed her on the lips and slowly began entering her, an inch at a time. When he was finally fully sheathed he took a deep breath. "I want you with me Sabrina. I'm not going to come until you do."

Slowly he began rocking back and forth. When he felt he was getting closer he moved his hand between them and rubbed her clit between his fingers. He leaned in and took one of her nipples into his mouth which triggered her orgasm. Feeling her go off, he picked up his rhythm and quickly followed her over the edge.

Slumped on top of her, Alex worked hard to gain control of his breathing. He gradually moved off of Sabrina and shifted onto his back. Pulling her close to him he kissed the top of her head as it lay on his shoulder.

"That was incredible baby. Get some rest for a while okay."

Sabrina barely managed a mumble before falling asleep on Alex's shoulder.

SABRINA SLOWLY BECAME AWARE OF A muscular hard thigh against her leg. She slowly turned her head and saw Alex's face, sound asleep. Oh dear God what have I done. Of all the stupid, irresponsible things. This should never have happened she fumed. He had caught her in a weak moment and look what happened!

She couldn't even blame the wine because she only had a few glasses. No, this was all on her! Now what to do?

Thinking quickly, Sabrina knew she couldn't be here when Alex woke up. Slowly she scooted to the edge of the bed, carefully extricating herself from Alex's arms. Eventually her feet hit the floor and she looked at Alex half expecting him to wake up. When she was assured that he hadn't been disturbed, she silently walked out to his living room and put her clothes on. Leaving without saying anything was so wrong on every level and Sabrina knew it. Taking out a pen from her purse and ripping a paper towel from the holder she wrote Alex a quick note then hastily left his apartment.

Chapter 16

A LEX ROLLED OVER AND STRETCHED, REACHING out his left arm for Sabrina. When his arm only found air he sat up and called out to her. When there was no answer he sat up in bed thinking she had probably just gone to the bathroom. He waited a few more minutes then swung his legs over the edge of the bed and stood up.

When he checked the bathroom and found that it was empty he headed out to the living room thinking she had just gotten up early and didn't want to wake him.

When he walked out, he looked around and, not seeing her on the couch, he looked on the floor and realized that her clothes were missing. Son of a bitch!

He turned towards the kitchen and saw a paper towel sitting on the breakfast bar with writing on it. Frowning he walked over and leaned over to read the note.

Alex,
Last night shouldn't have happened.
I'm sorry!
Sabrina

Seething, Alex went to find his cell phone to call her. They needed to talk about this and he'd be damned if he was going to let her go back to hiding. Last night had been incredible and he wasn't about to lose her because of some misguided need to keep people at a distance. Not after last night. Not after everything left between them. And he knew she felt it too, which was probably what had scared her.

Finding his phone he quickly ran through his directory; found her number and pushed send to dial. Her phone rang several times before going to her voicemail.Leaving a brief message thanking her for a wonderful night and asking her to return his call, he hung up.

Maybe it would be better if he just went to work and gave her some time and space. Thinking it would be a good idea he decided to send her some flowers and an offer to have dinner at a restaurant of her choice. That way she wouldn't feel any pressure on any expectations she might think he had.

Feeling better about the situation Alex went back to his bedroom to shower and get ready for work.

~

JESUS, MARY AND JOSEPH WHAT WAS I thinking Sabrina fumed as she entered her office. As wonderful as last night was, it should never have happened.

Sabrina slammed her briefcase on her desk and slumped in her chair. Think Sabrina, what are you going to do now? Alex had already called and left her a message and she knew that wasn't going to be the end of it.

Standing up she made her way over to her drawing table and sat down. Work…that was what she needed. Focus on something other than rock hard abs and….stop it Sabrina! Work!

It took a while but eventually she was able to focus on the project that needed her immediate attention. Several hours passed when Kat knocked on her door and entered her office with a vase filled with beautiful flowers.

"You have an admirer it would seem" she smiled.

Standing up and going over to the vase, Sabrina pulled the card out and read it to herself.

Thank you for an incredible evening.
How about dinner Friday night,
You pick the restaurant!
Yours,
Alex

"So what does it say" Kat asked. "Who are they from?"

Sabrina picked up the vase of flowers and handed them back to Kat. "Nobody. Why don't you put these out in the reception area okay?"

Kat took the flowers and frowned at Sabrina as she watched her stuff the card into her pocket. "Nobody went to a lot of expense for you."

"Kat, please, just do what I asked okay."

"Fine! What got you in a snit this morning?"

"I'm not in a snit" Sabrina said. Thinking quickly she continued, "I'm just stressed about this project. I think I'm going to have to drive down to Pittsburgh. They're having problems with the builder on that complex I designed for the Lassiter Brothers. He seems confused on some of the changes I made so I think it's better if I go down to meet with them personally."

"That's pretty sudden. I didn't know they were having issues. I can go Brie."

"No, thanks anyway. I think it's better if I go."

"What do you need me to do? I can get your flight taken care of and book you into a hotel and get you a rental car" Kat offered.

"I'm not flying Kat. I'm just not ready yet. It'll be a nice drive and I'll break it up by stopping in the Poconos for a night."

"When are you leaving" Kat asked.

"I'm not sure yet. I'll let you know shortly."

Walking over to her desk, Sabrina sat down and blew out a breath. Okay, so maybe they didn't really need her to be there in person but it might be a good thing to be there. The Lassiter Brothers would certainly be impressed by the personal attention they would be getting.

Knowing this decision just made her a big ole chicken, she picked up the phone anyway and dialed the number for The Lassiter Brothers. By the end of the conversation she had her arrangements set and two very happy clients. Packing up everything she thought she would need for the trip she made her way out to Kat's desk.

Kat looked up when Sabrina exited her office and, looking at the things in her hand raised her eyebrow. "What's going on?"

"I'm on my way out now Kat. I'm just heading home to pack a few things then I plan on hitting the road as soon as I can. I'll stay in the Poconos this evening and should be in Pittsburgh by Friday to meet with the contractor."

"Why not wait until after the weekend?"

"Well, I want to get a head start and have everything cleared up with the builder on Friday so construction can start again on Monday. Besides, it'll be nice to have the weekend to look around. Who knows, maybe I can even get a line on a few other jobs while I'm there!"

"Well, what hotels should I book? Where in the Poconos" Kat asked.

"I'll handle it. I'm not sure how far I'll get; it depends on how my legs do. I'll figure it out as I go."

"What's going on Sabrina? This last minute crap isn't like you. It's almost like you're running from something."

"I'm fine. Stop worrying. I'll call you this evening when I know where I'm staying, okay. Just keep working on the Dunns Project and if the hospital calls with their decision have them call me on my cell okay? Oh, and could you cover my shift for me for *Loving Hands*? I just have tomorrow night and everything else is covered."

Standing up and walking over to Sabrina, Kat put her arms around her and hugged tightly. "I don't know what's going on with you right now Brie, but I'm really worried. I won't push, but know if you need me all you have to do is call."

Sabrina had tears in her eyes when she pulled back. "Thanks Kat. I'll be in touch."

~

ALEX SLAMMED HIS HAND ON HIS kitchen counter in frustration. "Two weeks Sam" he yelled. "She's been gone for two damn weeks and she won't even return my calls."

Sam just grimaced as he watched his brother pace back and forth. He'd been worked up like this since Sabrina left and nothing seemed to calm him down. Sam tried taking him out to dinners, drinks after work and even challenged him to a no rules basketball game and still nothing appeased him.

"Alex, Kat says she's doing fine. They speak at least twice a day and she would know if something was wrong. You've heard of the Lassiter Brothers and know very well they're demanding, hard driving business men and things just took longer than she anticipated. Besides, from what Kat says, between their demands and the two new clients she's pursuing, she's been busy."

Okay, Sam thought that even sounded lame to his ears. He agreed with Alex that Sabrina could have at the very least called Alex to let him know that she was okay. You just don't make love to a man and leave him hanging like that with no explanation. Alex had seemed so happy that next morning when he came into work and said that he and Sabrina were working things out.

"Look man" Sam began. "Sabrina is supposed to be back at the end of next week and then I'm sure you two will sit down and work this thing out."

Alex just grunted and shook his head. "She shouldn't have driven all that way with her legs still weak. What if she'd gotten into a car accident? And what about working near the construction site with that damn stupid contractor that couldn't figure the drawings out? You know that the ground around the construction area is uneven. Is she being careful? I'd know the answer to those questions if she'd bother to take my calls!"

"Alex, you'd better get your temper under control before she gets back. You approach her with this attitude and she'll hand you your balls on a silver platter. She's a grown ass woman who won't take kindly to your interference in how she runs her life."

Taking a deep, calming breath Alex walked over to the windows overlooking the city skyline and looked out. "I know. I get what you're saying but I know in my heart that she left because of me and not some damn project that needed fixing."

Sam walked over and clamped his hand on Alex's shoulder. "I know this is hard Alex. Just take it easy and wait for her to get back. You can't push too hard or she'll run harder and faster away from you."

"I just don't understand why she's so afraid Sam."

Hesitating Sam took a deep breath and looked at his brother. "Look, Alex, Kat told me something about Sabrina's past that I think explains a lot. She told me this in confidence but it's something I think would help you to understand where she's coming from. You have to promise me though, that you'll not let either of the girls know I told you what happened. "

Alex turned to his brother, alarm in his eyes. "What happened?"

"Well, when Sabrina was younger she was dating this guy that her parents didn't like very much. Did you know that Kat originally worked for Sabrina's father? Well, anyway, Kat had gone to work one morning and evidently found Mr. Wallace in his office pretty upset. He'd spent the night at the hospital because Sabrina was taken there after this guy beat her up pretty badly. The guy was prosecuted but I guess he messed with Sabrina's head pretty badly while he was beating on her, saying that she deserved what she was getting, that she was nothing and he was leaving her because she wasn't worth his time."

"That son of a bitch" Alex fumed.

"I know. Unfortunately it gets worse. Sabrina was in therapy for a while and seemed to be getting better. Right before her parents died she started dating again and seemed to really like the guy. According to Kat, her Dad even thought he was a great guy and things were good. The day her parents died she was out on a date with him when she got the call. He took her to the hospital but it was already too late, both her mom and dad had passed. Sabrina had to indentify the bodies so they took her down to the morgue. After she came out the guy handed her coat to her and started to walk away. When Sabrina asked him where he was going, he told her he was leaving because it was too much drama to deal with. The cold hearted son of a bitch just left her standing there outside the morgue crying."

"Oh my God...."

"Kat said that after that she refused to date or to allow anybody to get close to her. Kat seems to be the one exception to her rule. You see Alex, even before the plane crash she had so much on her plate to deal with. Then that happened and to be honest, I just don't know what keeps her going. I know they say that God only gives us what we can handle but Jesus, she's had more than her fair share I think."

Stunned Alex walked over to the couch and sat down. He put his head in his hands and just sat there like that for a few minutes.

Sam came over and sat down beside him. "Alex, I confided in you for several reasons. One, I thought you should understand why Sabrina is running. I think she feels something for you but it scares the hell out of her. The second and most important reason is that given her past, I think you should really spend a little time thinking about what you want from her. If you're unsure about your feelings Alex walk away now. I worry about you but more so about her right now. She's been through a lot and I just don't know that she could take another rejection if you continued to pursue her then realized it wasn't what you wanted."

"I get what you're saying Sam."

"Look, I'll leave you alone for a while to think. Call me if you want some company okay?"

Alex stood up and hugged his brother. "Thanks Sam. I appreciate you telling me this."

"No problem."

After Sam left, Alex spent the next several hours sitting on his couch thinking about Sabrina and what Sam had told him. Whatever happened when she got back, he would have to tread lightly. Sam's advice was very true. He had to be sure of exactly what he wanted and he had exactly one week to figure it out, for both of their sakes.

~

As SABRINA LET HERSELF INTO HER apartment she felt relieved to be back. She'd decided to drive straight through instead of staying in the Poconos for a night. She was exhausted but very happy to be back in her apartment. Nothing like the comforts of home!

After unpacking her suitcase and making herself a cup of tea she sat down to go through her mail. Fortunately there wasn't anything of importance so she sat back, pulled the afghan from the back of her couch and covered up to watch TV. Feeling exhausted she promptly fell asleep.

It was her second day back at work before Alex tried calling her. In the beginning of her trip he called several times a day, always leaving a message. By the third day he only called once a day and by the end of the first week he had stopped all together. Although Sabrina tried to convince herself that it was for the best she missed his calls and knowing he was at least thinking of her.

Hearing a commotion out in the reception area, Sabrina got up from her desk and went around and opened her door. Alex swung around as the door opened and pinned her with a glare. "You and I need to talk."

"Alex now isn't a good time."

He stared hard at her for a few seconds, then simply walked past her and into her office. Sighing heavily she grimaced at Kat then followed Alex into her office shutting the door behind her.

Sabrina walked over to her office windows and leaned against the ledge watching as Alex paced around her office. He seemed to be trying to get his thoughts together when he stopped, looked at Sabrina, then walked over and pulled her into a tight hug. He let go after a few seconds and stepped back.

"You were gone a long time. I missed you. You look like hell."

"I had work to do Alex and thanks for that heartwarming compliment" she said sarcastically.

Pushing his hand through his hair Alex looked sheepishly at Sabrina. "I'm sorry. That didn't come out right. You just look tired Sabrina and I'm worried about you. I think we need to talk about what happened between us before you left."

"No we don't Alex. I told you, it should have never happened. Now I have work to get caught up on if you don't mind."

"I do mind. We need to talk about us. If you don't want to talk here how about we go out to dinner tonight and talk then."

"There is no US Alex. It was a one night stand. I had a lovely time but that's all there was to it."

Shocked Alex just stared at her. "I don't believe you."

"Look, I know you have a pretty big ego, after all you are a great looking guy, but there isn't anything going on between you and me. You were there for me during a really difficult time in my life but that's all there was Alex. I will be forever grateful but that's it. We're done."

"Sabrina, you don't have to do this. Believe it or not, not every man is a jerk that's going to leave you. Give me a chance to prove that to you."

"Alex, I'm good. Honestly. I told you, I'm not looking for a relationship."

Blowing out a breath Alex walked over to Sabrina and grabbed her arm turning her to face him. "Sabrina, I can't say this any plainer, I love you and I want us to be together. I can make you happy, I know I can."

Sabrina stared at him, tears gathering in her eyes. Hesitating for a few brief minutes, she pulled her arm from his grasp and walked over to her desk and sat down. "I think we're done here Alex. There isn't anything more to say."

Alex slammed his hand on her desk and leaned down and yelled at her. "This isn't over Sabrina. I'll give you more space if that's what you need but this isn't done. Not by a long shot!"

Alex walked out of Sabrina's office and slammed her door shut. Glancing over at Kat he shook his head and walked out of the office. Kat immediately got up and went over to Sabrina's door. Without knocking she went in and frowned down at Sabrina.

"Are you completely nuts" she yelled?

Wearily Sabrina stood up to gather her things. "Let it go Kat."

"No, I won't let it go. That man loves you and you're going to just let him go? This could be your chance at being happy Brie. Why are you turning away from him? My God, stop being so stubborn and take a chance!"

"Been there done that Kat. Didn't work out so well the last few times I tried it. No thanks. I prefer it on my own."

"You're a fool Sabrina" she said. Watching her pack things in her briefcase she added, "and what are you doing?"

"I'm heading home to work from there. I think I'm coming down with the flu."

"Can I get you anything?"

"No, I'm fine. I'll see you tomorrow."

Making sure she had anything she might need to work a few more hours from home, Sabrina set off towards her apartment.

Remembering that she still hadn't gone grocery shopping since she got back, she stopped in to the mini market a few blocks from her place to get a few things. She went through the aisles balancing her briefcase and a small basket adding anything that sounded good to her. Unfortunately after fifteen minutes her basket only contained chicken soup, saltine crackers and ginger ale. Not exactly a gourmet meal but it would have to do since it was the only thing that sounded good to her.

As she turned the next corner to head towards the checkout counter she bumped into a lady heading down the aisle she just exited.

"I'm so sorry" she began when she glanced up and realized that the lady she almost mowed down was none other than Elizabeth Deluca, Alex's mom.

Smiling broadly Elizabeth reached over and gave Sabrina a hug and a kiss on the cheek. "Oh honey, it's so nice to see you again."

Sabrina hugged her back then stepped away to look at her twinkling eyes. "It's nice to see you again too Mrs. Deluca. How are you? How's Mr. Deluca?"

"Everybody's doing fine honey. We were sorry you couldn't join us over the holidays. t would have been so nice to have you with us."

"I'm sorry. Things have just been crazy."

"I hear. I know Alex was worried about you being away for so long those few weeks." Glancing down at Sabrina's basket she looked back to her with concern on her face. "Are you feeling okay honey? Soup and crackers are usually what people who aren't feeling well eat."

"It's nothing. I just think I'm getting a touch of the flu, that's all."

Reaching over she put her hand against Sabrina's forehead. "I don't feel a fever dear. You do look a little pale though.

"I'm good. I'm just heading home to curl up on my couch and rest for a while."

"Can I do anything for you" Mrs. Deluca asked in concern.

"You're very sweet to ask but it's nothing. I'm just going to head home. It was so nice to see you again. Give Mr. Deluca my love okay?"

Squeezing Sabrina tightly she tapped Sabrina's cheek and told her to call if she needed anything.

Sabrina paid for her groceries and headed home to the warmth of her afghan and a nice long nap.

Chapter 17

ALEX WALKED INTO HIS PARENT'S HOUSE and hung his jacket up in the hall closet. He walked down the hall towards the kitchen yelling out for his mom. Mrs. Deluca poked her head around the corner with a smile on her face. "In here dear."

He walked over and gave him mom a hug. "Hi Mom. Thanks for the invite to dinner but what's the occasion?"

"Do I need a reason to have my boys here to eat with your Dad and me? Which reminds me, where's your brother? I thought you two would have come together."

Grabbing a cucumber from the salad that was sitting on the counter Alex popped it in his mouth before answering. "He's on his way. He said he had to stop by Kat's place to drop something off."

"Good. I was hoping that we could have a few minutes to chat before everybody got here."

"Sure, what's up? Who did what to whom that has you in a tizzy?"

Elizabeth smacked her sons hand as he reached into the salad bowl to snag something else. "I'm not in a tizzy. I've been worried about you and just wanted to have a talk." Placing a glass of iced tea in front of Alex she continued, "I just wanted to see how you're doing. You know, how's your brother working out, how's the company, how's your apartment, are you happy?"

"Mom.....has Sam been talking to you?"

Elizabeth looked up in surprise. "Sam? Please, he's as tight lipped as a clam. And believe me; I've tried everything to get him to tell me things from bribes of Red Velvet Cakes to offering to clean his apartment. He won't divulge a thing so I've decided to go right to the source!"

Laughing Alex reached out and grabbed his mother's hand. "Mom.... you do realize that Sam has someone that comes in to clean his place right? Besides, you don't need to go through Sam. I'll tell you whatever you want to know. I'm an open book."

"Since when" she asked incredulously. "Okay fine. So answer my questions."

"Well, Sam and I are doing great. He's working hard and I feel relief that he's stepped in. We spend a lot of time together outside work, when he's not with Kat that is. The company is doing fine. Business is great in fact, my apartment is my sanctuary and I still love it there and as far as being happy, well, I'm working on that."

"What do you mean by working on it?"

"It's complicated" Alex sighed.

"Complicated how? Please tell me you aren't still pursuing that Jessica girl. Now you know I try hard to stay out of my boys lives but seriously Alex, she's just....I don't know....self absorbed. You need to be with someone who thinks of someone other than themselves."

Smiling Alex reached over and rubbed his mom's shoulder. "It's not Jessica Mom. I'm in love with Sabrina and have been for a while now. She's not exactly making things easy at the moment and I just don't know how to convince her I'm not like all the other men she's been around."

Alex proceeded to update his mom on everything that had been happening including the information that Sam had given him on her past. "So you see Mom, I have to tread carefully because of everything I know. She's just so scared to let me in and I don't know how to break through that shell of hers. I'm worried about her."

"I ran in to her last week at that little mini mart I get that pasta salad I like at. She looked tired."

"Did you spend any time talking to her" Alex asked.

"Briefly. She wasn't feeling well, said she just stopped in for something to eat. When I looked in her basket she had soup and crackers. Said she thought she was coming down with the flu or something."

"What day was that Mom?"

"Tuesday I think. Why?"

"I saw her on Thursday. She was walking on the other side of the street when I noticed her. I didn't approach her because I said that I would give her more space. I'm still trying to figure out a way to get her to see reason." Alex looked over to his Mom. "If you have any suggestions or advice, I'll listen to anything. I'm getting desperate."

Elizabeth came around and put her arms around her son. "Just patience Love, she has a lot to overcome."

~

SABRINA MADE HER WAY THROUGH THE various headstones heading to where her parents were buried. It had been a while since she last came to see them. Sometimes, like today, she needed the peace that she found when she came to be near them.

For the past several weeks Sabrina had been rethinking her life and some of the choices she had made. It was fine to not want to be hurt but after spending time in the company of Kat and Sam she was beginning to realize what was missing from her life. Seeing them together, so happy and affectionate with each other made her want that same thing.

Last week she had seen Alex from across the street and it took a lot for her not to yell out his name to get his attention. He looked so handsome and seeing him brought back some of the nicer memories of the time they spent at his parent's Cape house. Being with him, having his unconditional support made what could have been a difficult recovery bearable.

Remembering what it was like to sleep in his arms the night they spent together still gave her goose bumps. He was a tender, considerate lover and she spent a lot of time thinking what it would be like if he were truly hers.

Reaching the gravesite of her parents, Sabrina kneeled down to pull some of the weeds that had grown around the headstone. After everything was cleaned up to her satisfaction, she sat in silence and stared at the names of her parents.

Oh Mom and Dad, I miss you both so much. I wish you were here to talk to me. I know that if you saw how I was living you wouldn't be happy with me. I know you taught me to love but I'm just so afraid that I'll get hurt again. Without you here, I just don't know if I could go through that disappointment alone. But oh if you met Alex I just know you would love him like I do.

Holy crap where did that come from? Love, Sabrina thought? Yes…I do love him she realized, more than life itself. Maybe that's why this was so scary. The feelings for Alex were so much more than they were for any guy she'd ever been with before. If there was devastation before, what would happen if Alex decided to leave too?

Sitting back on her heels Sabrina lifted her face to the breeze that was blowing gently across the cemetery. Inhaling the soft fragrance of a lilac tree she smiled. As far as she could tell there were two options. Walk away from Alex and spend the rest of her life as she had been, alone, or two, take a chance and possibly be able to spend the rest of her life with someone that she loved.

When she compared the two without letting anything from her past getting in the way, the choice was simple. What a fool I've been, she thought, trying to push him away just because she was too scared to take a chance. What an awful waste of time! Hadn't the plane crash taught her that life was too short?

What if it was too late? What if he's finally given up on me just when I've realized I want to take a chance with him she thought? I want a life with him!

Standing up Sabrina blew a kiss to her mother and father. *Goodbye for now mom and dad. Wish me luck because I'm off to go fight for a future with the man I love.* With a renewed purpose Sabrina walked back to her car and began the brief journey back to her apartment. She had plans to make!

$$\sim$$

SABRINA SPENT THE REST OF THAT night trying to figure out the best way to approach Alex. Deciding that she needed Kat and Sam's help she called them both and asked them to meet her in her office the next morning. If two heads were better than one, than certainly three heads would be even better. Besides, who better to get advice from than Alex's own brother?

Having gotten little sleep the night before, Sabrina was up early enough to stop at the local Dunkin Donuts to grab some bagels and coffee for everyone. After setting everything up in her office she sat at her desk and waited for them to arrive.

Finally at around 8:00 she heard the door to the front office open. After a few minutes Kat walked in to her office with a confused expression on her face. "What's going on Brie? You were very cryptic on the phone last night."

"Where's Sam?"

"He'll be here in a few. He's parking the car."

Sabrina stood up and walked over to where she set the coffee up. Getting a whiff of the strong brew she felt bile rise up in her throat and quickly backed away. Sitting back at her desk she took a few deep breaths hoping the nauseous feeling would fade.

"What's wrong Brie? You suddenly look really pale."

"Nothing. The coffee smell just got to me. I think I'm still fighting the flu."

Looking at her sideways Kat said, "Maybe you should go to the doctor. You've been fighting that bug since you got back from Pittsburgh."

The door to the outside office opened again and Sam walked in with a question on his face. "So what's going on Sabrina? Everything okay? You sounded strange on the phone last night."

Feeling a little lightheaded Sabrina took a few deep breaths to try to get her equilibrium back. "I need your help in figuring out the best way to get Alex."

"Excuse me" he asked.

"I've done a lot of soul searching and came to the realization that I've been a complete and utter fool in pushing him away. I need your advice on how to get him back."

"Oh honey" Sam laughed. "You never lost him. Just crook your little finger and believe me, he'll come running."

"About damn time" Kat harrumphed.

"You don't understand. I want to do something really special so he'll know that I love him with all of my heart and I'm not going to push him away anymore. He said he'd give me space but it's been over a week and I'm worried that he's given up on me. If what you say is true Sam, then I just want to do something so he knows how much he means to me."

Standing up and walking around her desk Sabrina caught the smell of the coffee once again. Fighting the urge to throw up she brought her hand to her mouth, swayed slightly and passed out cold.

~

SABRINA OPENED HER EYES AND FOUND two concerned faces staring at her. Looking around she realized that she was lying on the couch across from her desk. Sam kept touching her forehead and Kat was rubbing her legs.

"What happened" Sabrina asked.

"You started walking over to us, got really pale, weaved a little then passed out. Sam got to you before you hit the floor and carried you over to here. I was just going over to call an ambulance when you started coming around."

"No, no ambulance. I'm fine, really. That's just strange. I've never passed out before in my life."

Sam shook his head. "You really should let us call the ambulance. You scared the shit out of me and I don't like how pale you are."

Shifting her legs to the floor so she could sit up, Sabrina touched her head and looked at Kat. "Must be this flu bug I've been fighting."

"Well, if you won't let us call an ambulance" Sam started, "then we're taking you to the hospital ourselves."

Sabrina started to argue then decided against it. Kat had that determined look on her face so she knew there would be no mercy for her until a doctor took a look at her. Besides, she hadn't been feeling well for a while so it was just as well.

Sam took his keys from his pocket and looked at Kat. "I'm going to get my car and pull it up front. You two meet me downstairs in ten minutes okay? Do you feel well enough to make it down" Sam asked.

"I'm fine Sam. Thanks. Just give us ten minutes." Then putting her hand on Sam's arm she looked up at him. "Don't call Alex, okay Sam. I don't want the first time I reach out to him to be because something's wrong okay?"

Hesitating Sam shook his head. "I won't….unless something's really wrong okay? Then I will call him and you won't be able to talk me out of it. Got it?"

Sabrina nodded yes then Sam left to go downstairs to get the car. Kat took a hold of Sabrina's hand.

"Brie, how long have you been feeling nauseous and lightheaded?"

Thinking back Sabrina said "Maybe two, three weeks. Why?"

"And certain things trigger it like the smell of coffee?"

"That and other things. Why? What are you getting at?"

"Good Lord Brie, think about it. Nauseous, lightheaded, you've been pretty tired lately. When was the last time you had a period?"

"I don't…..well it's been….."

"Since before you and Alex made love?"

"Kat, I've been on birth control for over a year now. There's no way" Sabrina said shocked.

"Well, let's not panic or assume anything. Let's just head to the hospital and get you checked out. I think you should tell the doctor that you suspect that you may be pregnant though, okay?"

THE RIDE TO THE HOSPITAL WAS made in silence. Sabrina kept going back to the last few weeks and started feeling pretty ridiculous for not even suspecting she may be pregnant. The flu indeed! She hadn't even thought to ask Alex to wear a condom. She knew she was on the pill, and that medically she was clean. Knowing what type of man Alex was she wasn't worried about him being clean but that probably wasn't a smart assumption these days.

Sam arrived at the hospital and dropped her and Kat off at the emergency room entrance, saying he would meet them in the waiting room. One of the doctors that Sabrina knew pretty well from her *Loving Hands* organization recognized her and walked over to her to greet her and ask why she was there. After explaining that she was at work and had passed out he frowned and stood up taking a hold of her arm.

"Why don't you come with me and we'll get you checked out."

Sabrina followed him back to the examining room and sat down. She was given paperwork to fill out and once that was completed and she answered the questions they had for her, she mentioned that it could be a possibility that she was pregnant. She patiently sat while they poked and prodded and drew blood. After about forty-five minutes later the doctor came back in to speak to her and confirmed that yes, she was definitely pregnant. He expressed concern that her sugar level wasn't where it should be and gave her the name and number of an obstetrician he wanted her to go see.

"I know by your medical records on file that you're primary care physician has been taking care of your yearly pap smears but you need more specialized care now, particularly with the concern with your sugar levels. Call that number and make an appointment today okay?"

"I will. Should I be doing anything right now?"

Smiling the doctor patted her arm. "Look, I know this is a little overwhelming right now. Unless I miss my guess, this is coming as a shock to you. Don't worry. Just make that appointment and rest as much as you can. Make sure you eat, even if it's many smaller meals as opposed to several large ones. Now, I have two friends of yours pacing in my waiting room. Do you want me to send them back? They seem pretty worried."

"Sure."

Five minutes after the doctor had exited the room, Kat and Sam walked in with worried frowns on their faces.

Kat came over to sit on the bed next to Sabrina and Sam leaned against the opposite wall. Taking Sabrina's hand she asked, "Well?"

Sabrina looked at them both then. "I can't believe I'm saying this but….I'm pregnant."

Katherine jumped up and grabbed Sabrina in an exuberant hug. "Oh honey I'm so excited for you! This is fantastic news!"

Sam just laughed and cautioned Kat to stop jostling Sabrina around or she'd pass out again. Then he walked over to Sabrina and took her hand. "How're you feeling about all this Sabrina?"

"I just don't know what to think. I'm thrilled, I'm scared, and I'm worried about how Alex is going to take this. Oh my God!! Alex."

"Sabrina" Sam began, "I know my brother and believe me, he's going to be thrilled.

"Sam, you and Kat have to promise me that you won't say anything to him. I need to see how he feels about me first, before he knows about the baby." Grabbing both of their hands she pleaded with them both. "I'm serious, the only way we have a chance is for me to know that first and foremost he loves me, wants a future with me. Once I know that, I'll tell him about the baby."

Frowning Sam agreed. "Fine, I won't say anything but you need to do it soon. Alex deserves to know about his child sooner rather than later. And you deserve to have someone take care of you."

Smiling, Sabrina hugged Sam then Kat and hopped off the bed. "I need to get dressed now. I have a plan to work on."

As Sam and Kat walked to the door to leave Sabrina called out. "Hey Sam." When Sam turned around she said, "You didn't even ask me if it really was Alex's baby" she said smiling.

Sam just smiled back. "Please....you're as crazy about him as he is you. Kat and I figured that one out a while ago. It just took you two boneheads longer to figure it out."

Chapter 18

SABRINA GOT UP EARLY SATURDAY MORNING to the sun shining in her window and directly in her eyes. Smiling to herself she put her hand on her stomach, thinking of Alex's child.

It was so strange to think of being pregnant. It hadn't really been something she ever thought about. Her life had already been mapped out as far as she was concerned, and not only had it not included being with someone special, it certainly hadn't included a baby.

After the initial panic she felt when she got home Friday evening, the idea of a child of her own to love began to grow on her in a way she never thought was possible. Yes, Alex could get angry or panic and walk away from her but knowing she would have a piece of him helped to make that thought more bearable. He could walk out on her, but she would always have this child to love and care for. She was determined that no matter what happened with Alex, she would love and care for this baby with everything she had. There wouldn't be a day that went by that he or she wouldn't know how loved and wanted they were!

Sabrina lay in bed for a few hours longer, thinking of the baby and Alex and waiting for the nauseous feeling to subside. Eventually, feeling like she could move without throwing up, she threw the covers off her legs and slowly got out of bed.

After spending her morning puttering around her apartment she eventually got showered and dressed and headed out do a little shopping. Sabrina spent the entire day out, having lunch, looking around a few baby shops and even looked at some maternity clothes. Deciding to make the day even more special, she stopped in to a nail salon and treated herself to a manicure and pedicure, and then stopped on her way back home for her favorite take out of Chinese food.

Kicking back on her comfy couch with her food containers around her, fleece blanket on her legs and her favorite movie *The Towering Inferno* in the DVD player, Sabrina settled in for an evening of sheer bliss.

Later that night as she got ready for bed, Sabrina thought about the day and realized that this was probably the happiest day she had had since her parents passed away. Snuggling down into the covers she smiled to herself. Tomorrow she would work on her plan to get Alex back and then hopefully, this would only be the first of many happy days to come.

~

SABRINA ANXIOUSLY WAITED FOR THE ELEVATOR to arrive at the floor where Alex's office was. After spending all of Sunday trying to come up with a plan, she decided that she would surprise him in his office Monday after he got back from lunch, and ask him to have dinner with her. Because of Sam's help, she knew Alex was back from lunch because he called her when Alex's secretary called him. She headed right over as soon as the call came.

The elevator arrived with a ping and Sabrina walked over to the desk outside his office. Unfortunately no one was there so she decided to go to Alex's door and knock. As she got closer to the partially opened door she heard a female voice. Sabrina almost walked away when she heard the voice say, "I've missed you Alex."

Knowing it probably wasn't the smartest thing to do, she stepped closer to hear what his response was.

"Look Jessica, we were over a long time ago. I keep telling you that, but you don't seem to listen to me."

"Ah, come on Alex. We used to be good together" the voice whined.

"Jessica, seriously, we went out for a while, but you and I both know that it wasn't that good or we wouldn't have split up."

Sabrina smiled to herself. Poor Alex, he sounded like this was the last conversation he wanted to have. Deciding to rescue him she pushed his door open further, only to find that Jessica had grabbed his head and was kissing him like her life depended on it. Alex on the other hand was trying valiantly to push her away with one arm and disentangle her arms from around his neck with the other.

Keeping a straight face Sabrina cleared her throat loudly. When the two quickly separated she purposely frowned and said "Am I interrupting anything."

Alex stepped away from Jessica rubbing the back of his hand across his mouth. He frowned once at her then took a step away from her.

"This isn't what you think Sabrina."

"And what is it you think I think Alex?"

"Sabrina" the lady screeched. "So you're the woman trying to get her claws in my man. Seriously, do you think that pathetic helpless plane crash victim act will help you to keep Alex at your side?"

"I'm not sure what you're referring to" Sabrina stated, "but I'm here for a meeting with Alex. You can have your man back after our meeting."

After staring each other down for a few seconds, Jessica harrumphed, grabbed her purse and flounced to the office door. Before completely exiting, she turned and blew Alex a kiss. "I'll call you later honey" and out the door she went.

~

Alex looked at Sabrina, trying to judge her reaction to the scene that just played out in his office. Of all the times for Jessica to stop by his office and try her attempt at reconciliation, this had to have been the worst. He was on murky ground as it was with Sabrina and this may have just ruined any chance he may have had with her.

Alex stepped towards Sabrina pushing his fingers through his hair in frustration. "Look, Sabrina, that wasn't what it looked like. Jessica stopped by......."

Smiling Sabrina shook her head. "Relax Alex. I heard what you were saying to her before I came in."

Hesitating Alex looked to Sabrina. "You heard? You're not mad then? You know that I wasn't trying to get back with Jessica?"

Sabrina walked over and sat in one of the chairs in front of Alex's desk. Following her lead Alex walked around to his desk and sat in his chair and scooted it forward. Placing his arms on the desk in front of him he looked at Sabrina.

"I'm glad you heard but I'm still sorry you walked in on that. So what brings you here? Not that I'm not happy to see you because I am. Is everything okay? Are YOU okay?"

"I'm fine Alex. I just wanted to ask you something."

"Anything you want, name it."

"Dinner."

"Excuse me" Alex asked?

"Dinner" Sabrina repeated. "I'd like to have dinner with you. Whenever you have time. Tuesday, Wednesday....."

"Tonight" Alex interrupted.

"Tonight?"

"Look, I've been trying to get you to spend time with me for a while. If you're asking I'm accepting!"

Shaking her head Sabrina stood up. "Perfect, tonight then. Where do you want to go?"

"Would I be pushing my luck if I asked you to have dinner at my place" Alex asked.

"No Alex, you wouldn't be pushing your luck. Dinner at your place sounds lovely. Can I bring anything?"

"Nope, I've got it covered. How about I pick you up at 6:00 then we can stop and grab some take out on the way back to my place."

"Sounds like a plan. See you then Alex."

As she made her way to his office door, Alex came around from his desk and gently took a hold of her elbow and turned her back to him. "Is everything okay Brie?"

Sabrina looked up at Alex and smiled. "Yes, Alex, everything is just great. I'll see you later okay?"

Dumbfounded Alex mumbled okay and watched as she made her way to the elevator.

Several minutes later Sam rounded the corner to Alex's office only to find him still standing outside his office staring at the elevator.

"Something wrong Alex? You're staring at that elevator like you're expecting it to open and the devil himself to walk out."

Shaking his head Alex turned and walked back in to his office. Sam followed him in and plunked down on the couch across from the desk.

"Sabrina was just here."

Sam smirked and waited for Alex to give him more details.

"Yeah, she came in when Jessica was here and caught us kissing."

"What the hell..." Sam yelled as he jumped to his feet. "She must be really pissed right now. How could you Alex! And with that tramp...."

"Relax" Alex said. "Sabrina evidently heard some of the conversation I had with Jessica before she walked in, telling her we were through, and she saw that I was pushing Jessica away, not encouraging the kiss."

Sitting back down Sam exclaimed "thank God. So what did she say?"

Alex looked at Sam with a grin on his face. "We're having dinner together. Tonight."

"Any idea why" Sam interjected.

"No idea whatsoever. She seemed kind of...I don't know.....at peace. I asked her if anything was wrong but she said she was fine. I mean, she looked fine to me. Maybe a little tired and pale but she just seemed... calmer. I don't know how to explain it."

"Well" Sam started, "I guess you'll find out tonight won't you." Standing up Sam walked over to the door. "Good luck tonight man. I hope things work out for you."

"Thanks Sam. I'll see you tomorrow."

"Heading out now? You have a few more hours before the dinner."

"I know" Alex said laughing."I'm heading over to Mom's to beg her to make a dinner for me."

"You're pathetic" Sam laughed as he closed the door.

Alex thought he heard Sam say something about a mamma's boy before he shut the door completely, but at this point Alex didn't care. He needed tonight to be special and he was willing to do anything and con anyone into helping him that he could think of. Besides, knowing his mom loved Sabrina like a daughter, he knew she wouldn't mind helping him out.

~

SABRINA AGONIZED OVER WHAT TO WEAR for over an hour before she decided on a simple wrap around dress in black and white. Black pumps with a small heel and diamond earrings and she was ready to go.

Gathering her coat and purse she was heading out to her kitchen when there was a knock at her door. She went over to look out the peephole and saw Alex standing on the other side. Opening her door she grinned at him.

"How did you get in the main door without me buzzing you in?"

"I helped some nice lady in with her groceries" Alex grinned.

"Evidently security needs to be tightened around here."

"Evidently" he smirked. "Ready to go?"

Alex took Sabrina's coat and held helped her in to it. Taking her keys from her, he locked the door on the way out and held her arm as they walked down the stairs and out to his car.

The drive to his apartment was slower than Alex wanted, but the traffic was a little heavy. He'd waited all day to have this time with Sabrina; he could certainly be patient a little while longer.

He spent the rest of the day after he left his Mom's house thinking about her and wondering why she had asked for the dinner. After months of trying to get her to come around he was worried and anxious about what she might have to say to him. On one hand, if it were bad, she just wouldn't have contacted him would she? On the other hand, maybe she just wanted to see him face to face to tell him to move on and stop hoping she would change her mind.

Deciding that he wouldn't know until he heard it straight from her what this dinner was about, he spent the time waiting until 6:00 picking up his apartment and visiting with his Mom as she made their dinner.

A few minutes later, hoping his Mom had finished and left his apartment; Alex unlocked his door and stepped aside to allow Sabrina to walk in.

Alex helped her out of her coat and hung it up in the closet with his. Heading into the kitchen he asked her if she wanted a glass of wine.

"No thanks. I'd love some juice or iced tea if you have any. If not, water would be good."

Oh this can't be good, he thought. If she's trying to keep a level head by not having alcohol, whatever she had to say must be bad.

Going to the refrigerator he looked to see what he had. "Cranberry juice okay?"

"Sure."

After pouring her juice and a glass of wine for himself he walked over to where she was standing in the living room.

"Dinner smells really good Alex. I can't believe you had time to cook. I thought we were doing takeout."

Sheepishly Alex grinned. "I have to confess."

Sabrina raised her eyebrows.

"Mom came over and cooked for us."

"You're kidding, right?!?"

"No, I wanted something a little more special than takeout so I asked Mom to help me out. Chicken Kiev is one of her best dishes!"

Laughing Sabrina lightly punched Alex's arm. "I can't believe you made her come over and cook for you."

"For us, not me. Which by the way, it's ready so why don't we sit down and eat then we can talk. Okay?"

"Works for me. I'm starving."

'Good" Alex said. "You don't look like you've been eating very much lately."

Rolling her eyes, Sabrina helped Alex get the food on the table then sat down to eat. As dinner progressed they talked about how their jobs were going and about Alex's parents and Sam and Kat. Eventually they made their way through dessert when Sabrina pushed her chair back with a smile and patted her belly. "That was wonderful Alex but I'm stuffed."

"Good. Why don't you get comfortable on the couch and I'll load the dishwasher and join you."

"I can help."

Handing her the rest of her cranberry juice and gently shoving her towards the living room Alex declined her offer. "Got it covered. Relax and I'll be right there."

Sabrina went in to the living room and sat on the couch looking out at the city skyline. Quickly though, her head began to bob and soon she fell asleep with her head resting on her arm that was propped on the arm of the couch.

Alex watched as she drifted off to sleep. Walking over he pulled the afghan from the back of the couch and covered her up. He went back to the kitchen and finished cleaning up. When he was through he went back to the living room and turning the lights down low he went back to the couch and gently took Sabrina's feet and put them in his lap. He watched her sleep for a few minutes before picking up a book he had been reading and left on his end table. For the next hour Alex alternated between watching her sleep and reading his book.

Sabrina lifted her head up and looked around in confusion. Feeling warm she looked to the other end of the couch and realized that her feet were in Alex's lap and that he was smiling at her.

"Oh my God, I fell asleep. How long was I out?"

Alex rubbed her leg gently. "About an hour."

Sabrina drew her feet from his lap and onto the floor. Rubbing her eyes she apologized to him. "I'm so sorry Alex. I didn't mean to do that."

"Don't worry about it. You must have needed the rest."

Sabrina stood up and walked over to the window, trying to shirk the fog that was surrounding her. She was nervous enough with what she wanted to say to Alex and falling asleep was not the way she wanted to start off this conversation. If he was going to reject her, she needed to have her wits about her to handle it with grace, then leave quickly. Feeling tired and groggy was not a good start!

Alex stood up and followed her to the window. Rubbing her back he spoke gently to her.

"Look, Sabrina, you obviously have something on your mind. No matter what it is I promise it'll be okay. Just talk to me…please."

Sighing Sabrina pushed her hair behind her ears and looked at him. "Oh Alex, I've made such a mess of things."

Taking her hand Alex led her over to the couch and pushed her to sit down. When she wouldn't look at him he took her face by the chin and turned her to face him. Noticing she had tears in her eyes, he wiped them gently away. "Tell me what's wrong, sweetheart."

Taking his hand in hers she placed it in her lap and held on. After a few minutes, and a few deep breaths, she looked up and in to his eyes. "I'm such a coward Alex. I've spent so much of my life since my parents died pushing people away trying to convince myself that I didn't need or want anybody in my life. I did pretty good with that too until you came along. You made me want things that I'd convinced myself I didn't want or deserve. Honestly, I had it all figured out and now I know I was just full of crap. I got so bogged down with being scared and not wanting anybody to get close enough to hurt me that I actually had myself convinced that being alone was better. I mean, really, how moronic is that!" Agitated, Sabrina let go of Alex's hand stood up and walked back to the window. Turning to Alex she continued.

"I mean seriously, how screwed up am I? But I want you to know Alex that now that I have this figured out I understand if this is all too much for you to handle. I don't expect that, just because I finally got me figured out, that you would naturally feel the same way. Because I want you to know Alex that I'm stronger now than I have ever been in my life and I can handle it if you don't want this."

Alex got up from the couch and went over to Sabrina as she continued talking. "To be honest I mean who would. It's not like you would want to take on an emotionally deranged female" she babbled on "and as much as......"

"Stop" Alex said forcefully. When he had Sabrina's attention he smiled. "Three words Sabrina. That's all I want to hear from you, three little words."

Sabrina hesitated a few minutes, realizing he was smiling, and knew the exact three words he wanted to hear.

"I love you" she whispered.

"Thank God" he said before he picked her up and swung her around squeezing her tightly. "Thank God" he whispered setting her feet back on the floor and claiming her lips in a possessive kiss.

Chapter 19

SOMETHING WAS TICKLING ALEX'S NOSE WHICH was what caused him to wake up. Glancing at the clock on his nightstand he saw that it was a little after three in the morning. Feeling the warm body that was snuggled up against him, he realized that Sabrina was in his bed, in his arms, and it was her hair that was tickling his nose. It hadn't been a dream after all!

Smiling, he pulled her tighter to him and pushed his nose in her hair, smelling the soft fragrance that was uniquely hers. He still couldn't believe that she was with him and that she said she loved him. There were times when he worried that she would never get to the point of allowing him in. Although he had no idea what made her change her mind, he was grateful she did, and vowed that he would make sure she never regretted the decision that brought them together.

Sabrina sighed then rolled over on her side away from Alex. Gently he rolled to face her and put his arm around her waist and pulled her naked body up against his chest. Not able to resist, he brought his hand up and cupped her breast. He rolled her nipple between his fingers and admired the way it came to a peak, begging for more attention.

Gently his hand moved from her breast and slid down her ribs, past her flat stomach and through the feminine curls and on to her most private parts. Humming a soft sigh Sabrina lifted her leg and placed it on Alex's thigh, giving him more open access. When he leaned closer to kiss her cheek, he realized that she was still sound asleep. It humbled him to know that even in her sleep she trusted him enough to open up to him like that.

As he continued to use his fingers to stimulate her, Sabrina gradually began to stir. Alex nuzzled her neck as he continued his assault on her senses. Eventually he got his wish when Sabrina turned her head towards him and smiled. "Alex, what are you doing?"

"If you have to ask I must not be doing it right" he laughed.

Quickly Sabrina moved her leg off of him and turned so that they were both face to face as they lay in bed. Taking his face between her hands she kissed him passionately on the lips. When she pulled away, still holding on to him and looking into his eyes, she stared earnestly for a few seconds. "I meant what I said Alex. I love you, with everything I have. I won't let you go again."

Alex kissed her back then smiled at her as he pulled away. "And I won't let you go again either baby."

Sabrina watched him for a few seconds longer then laughed and pushed him on to his back. Climbing on top of him, she straddled his legs then looked down to his straining erection bobbing between them. "Hmmm...looks like you have a problem."

Alex laughed and looked up at the beautiful woman on top of him. "You seem to have that effect on me."

"Well maybe I can help you out with that" Sabrina laughed as she carefully rose up a little to position herself over his erection.

"Don't Brie" Alex hesitated. "I need you to be ready too. I don't want to hurt you."

"Oh Alex, I was ready the minute you touched me."

As she lowered herself onto him he breathed out a huff of air. Slowly she took him in, an inch at a time, until he was completely sheathed inside her. "Sweet Jesus, you feel so good baby."

Smiling, Sabrina leaned down and took Alex's hands and brought them to her breasts. As he started kneading them she began to ride him, slowly at first then picked up her pace as she felt her climax getting closer. Alex let go of her breasts and held up his hands. "Take my hands and I'll hold you steady baby."

Sabrina took a hold and watched his face as together they set a rhythm that quickly hurled them both into that incredible explosion of sheer bliss and fulfillment.

When they both started coming back into reality, Sabrina realized she was draped over Alex's chest, breathing heavily. Alex gently rolled them both to one side and pulled out of her. Disappearing for a few seconds, he came back with a cloth to clean them both up. Tossing it aside he crawled back into bed and pulled Sabrina back against his chest. "Sleep sweetheart" he whispered and they both drifted back into oblivion.

~

THE NEXT MORNING SABRINA WAS AWAKE before Alex and slipped out of bed quickly to head to his kitchen. Hoping to find a few saltine crackers to ease the nauseous feelings that plagued her in the mornings, she rummaged quietly through his cabinets. Finally in the last cabinet she opened, she found what she needed and took several crackers out and went to sit on the couch.

After nibbling on a few she took a deep breath and leaned her head back on the couch. She just needed to get through this morning without him finding out about her pregnancy. Praying to the powers above to just give her until tomorrow, she finished the last cracker then promptly ran to the guest bathroom and threw up.

After several minutes she washed her face and rinsed her mouth out then headed back to the living room. Fortunately Alex was still sleeping so she got a glass of water and went to stand by the windows to watch as the city began to wake up.

Hearing feet pattering on the floor, Sabrina looked towards the hallway as a sleepy, grumpy looking Alex practically jogged into the living room. She watched as he stopped short and quickly perused the kitchen area then the living room until his eyes landed on her by the windows. Sighing deeply he rubbed his eyes. "I thought you left."

Oh Alex, she thought, what have I done? Walking over to him she put her arms around his waist and laid her head on his chest, listening to his heart pounding. "I promise Alex, no more running. I'm here and I'm not going anywhere."

After a brief hesitation Alex put his arms around her and squeezed her to him. Kissing the top of her head he pulled away. "Good. Want some coffee" he asked.

"God no" she blurted before she could stop herself.

Alex raised an eyebrow at her. "You used to drink coffee. Swear off the caffeine" he laughed.

"Something like that" she mumbled.

"How about some breakfast. Eggs, toast, bagels?"

"Nothing thanks. I think while you're having breakfast I'll just jump in your shower if that's okay. I need to get to work by 9:00 this morning for a meeting."

Alex strolled over to Sabrina and pulled her into his arms. "You're welcome to my shower any time sweetheart. After you I'll jump in then I'll drop you off at your apartment to change then drop you at work.

"Alex, you don't need to take me to work. Just drop me at my place to change and I can get myself to work."

"Nope, I'll drop you off then pick you up at the end of the day." Hesitating for a few seconds, Alex pulled back and stared down at Sabrina. "I'd like you to spend tonight with me too. Maybe we can grab some take out and just relax here. We could stop by your place to get a few things so you won't have to worry about going back there before work tomorrow. "

Laughing Sabrina stood up on her tiptoes and kissed Alex. "Sounds like a plan, as long as you leave your mother alone and we really grab take out."

"That's a deal."

Sabrina walked out of her office later that morning to find Kat standing in the main entrance with a smile on her face. Stepping aside she revealed a beautiful bouquet of hydrangea's in a large vase sitting on the table by the couch in reception.

"Flowers for you and judging by the size of the arrangement, things must have gone well with you and Alex last night" Kat laughed.

Sabrina walked over and took out the card that was attached.

Thanks for a wonderful night and
for still being there this morning.
I love you!
Alex

Hugging the card to her chest she looked at Kat and smiled. "It was everything I wanted it to be and more. I really love him Kat."

Kat drew Sabrina into a tight hug. "I'm so happy for you kiddo. You deserve some happiness. Did you tell him about the baby?"

Stepping back Sabrina shook her head. "Not yet. I wanted to wait until I figured out if we had a chance as just us first. I plan on telling him tomorrow. I have my first doctor's appointment on Thursday and thought he might want to go with me. If he doesn't run, that is."

"Oh Brie, he's not going to run."

"I hope not, but it has to be his choice Kat. This is a big step and not one that we planned. I have no idea if kids are even anything he ever wanted. I'm not assuming anything at this point."

"Have a little faith Sabrina. Things will work out."

ALEX POPPED INTO SAM'S OFFICE SHORTLY before lunch. Tossing the jacket that was lying on the chair in front of his desk he said "Let's go flyboy."

Sam frowned then took the jacket in his lap and tossed it back across his desk and into the chair. "Not now Alex, I have work to do."

Realizing how funny it was that their positions had completely reversed, Alex bent over laughing.

"What's so funny" Sam frowned.

"You are. Wasn't it not too long ago you were saying something to me about working too much and being a dull boy?"

"Cut the crap Alex. I don't have time for this. I have two proposals to get out and a conference call this afternoon that I can't get out of."

"Well that's a shame Sam because I was hoping you would help me pick out an engagement ring and maybe after that we could pop in on our girls at work and take them some lunch. But hey, I understand if that paperwork is more important to you."

Sam looked up at Alex with a huge grin on his face. "Engagement ring huh? So things went pretty well last night?"

"What can I say....she loves me."

"Wow! Like the rest of us didn't already know that."

"Seriously, can you get away for a while to come with me?"

Jumping up from his seat Sam grabbed his jacket and pulled it on. "I'll make it work. This is important. Besides, seeing Kat will be a bonus."

"Didn't you just see her last night? Not getting bored?"

"What can I say man. She just does it for me. So, are you asking her to marry you today at lunch?"

"No, just getting it in my hand so I can pop the question when the timing is right. Maybe dinner one night this week. I don't want her to feel pressured or to feel that I'm moving too quick."

"Too quick" Sam laughed. "If this is you two moving too quick I'd hate to see your slow and thoughtful."

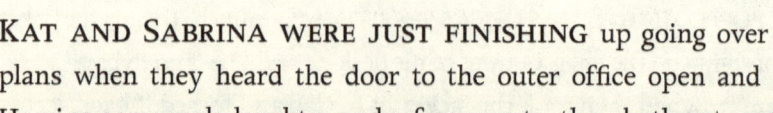

KAT AND SABRINA WERE JUST FINISHING up going over some plans when they heard the door to the outer office open and close. Hearing some male laughter and a few grunts, they both got up to see what was going on out in the reception area.

Alex and Sam both looked up when they heard the girls come out. Each of the guys had a grin on his face and a small bouquet of roses in their hands and brown bags with food.

Sam took the initiative first and walked over to Kat. "Hey doll face" he said as he handed her the flowers and dipped her into a hearty kiss.

Alex walked over to Sabrina smiling and handed her the flowers. "I missed you" he whispered and kissed her softly. "We brought you girls some lunch. Do you have time for a quick bite?"

Sabrina pulled away from Alex and grabbed for the brown bag. "Oh gimme....I'm starved."

Laughing Alex held it up high and motioned towards the conference room. Sam and Kat followed them in and helped to set everything up.

An hour later, having eaten everything they brought, the guys departed in time for Sam to take his conference call.

As the day wore on Sabrina spent a lot of her time sitting at her desk thinking about how happy she was feeling. Being with Alex just seemed so natural. Her heart felt lighter than she could ever remember. Just thinking that soon Alex would there to pick her up made her feel giddy and excited. If she could just figure out a way to tell Alex about the baby without freaking out, life would really be good.

TUESDAY EVENING WAS SPENT WITH BOTH Sabrina and Alex enjoying a delicious Italian dinner they picked up on the way home from work. Later, snuggling together on the couch, they watched the news then searched for a movie that they both could agree on and relaxed, quietly watching TV.

At some point Sabrina became bored with the movie and started torturing Alex by sliding her hand up his leg or licking his ear. After several attempts to motivate him to stop watching TV, she eventually gave up being subtle and just stood up, stripped her clothes off and looked at Alex.

"I'll be in the bedroom" she said and just walked away. Alex watched, stunned as Sabrina left the room, her behind jiggling in that enticing way that had him drooling. Not being one to be left behind, Alex jumped to his feet and followed her in.

~

IT SEEMED LIKE SABRINA HAD JUST fallen asleep when she felt Alex stirring behind her. Looking at the clock she realized that it was morning and that she had pretty much fallen fast asleep after they had made love last night. Surprisingly she hadn't stirred at all through the night.

Turning her head she saw that Alex was wide awake watching her. Smiling she rubbed his cheek. "Good morning."

"Good morning baby. How are you feeling?"

"Ummm….fine" she answered hoping the telltale signs of her usual morning nauseous bouts stayed at bay, long enough for her to tell him about the baby. This was the time, she thought, now or never.

"That wasn't very convincing. Everything okay" Alex asked.

Sabrina rolled so she was facing Alex completely. "Actually, I have something I want to tell you Alex" she began.

Alex smiled at her, then sat up. "Hold that thought baby. I have something for you." Reaching in to his nightstand, Alex pulled out the ring box he placed there last night and turned towards Sabrina. "I want you to move in here with me Sabrina. I want us to be together, all the time." He opened the ring box and reached out to give it to her. "Will you marry me Sabrina?"

Alex watched as Sabrina first looked at him with shock on her face, then horror. Thinking he misread the situation he snapped the lid shut and reached out to her.

"Oh Alex…" Sabrina began then bolted from the bed and ran into his bathroom.

Seconds later Alex heard her throwing up. Worried for her, he followed her in and saw her down on her knees in front of the toilet throwing up. Alex grabbed a wash cloth and dampened it with cold water then kneeled beside her. Pulling her hair into a ponytail with his hand he gently laid the cloth on the back of her neck.

Sabrina threw up a few more times then tried to stand up on shaky legs. Alex reached out and helped her up. Grabbing the toothbrush she put in his bathroom last night, he put toothpaste on it and handed it to her to brush. After she was through, he took a hold of her hand and led her back into the bedroom. Sitting her on the bed, he pulled a blanket around her shoulders and took a hold of her hand and sat beside her.

"So what was it that you wanted to tell me" he smiled.

Chapter 20

SABRINA LOOKED AT ALEX AND BUSTED out crying. Alex patiently handed her a kleenex from his nightstand and held her while she cried. Finally after several moments, she got control of herself and stood up to put some space between her and Alex.

Turning to face him she just hung her head, playing with the kleenex still in her hand. "I'm so sorry Alex. I didn't mean for this to happen. Honestly, I know that sounds so stupid and immature but I really wasn't trying to force you into anything by getting pregnant. I've been on birth control for years now and never thought for one instant that this would happen. I thought we were protected Alex, I honestly did."

Alex stood up and walked over to Sabrina. Taking her hand in his he tilted her head up and smiled. "Sabrina, if I was really dead set against having a child don't you think I would have taken some precaution myself?" Sighing heavily he grabbed her hand. "Come with me."

Alex led her out to the living room and had her sit on the couch. Going into the kitchen he grabbed her some juice and joined her on the couch. "Drink this."

Sabrina took a few long sips and put the glass down. "Feeling better" Alex asked?

"I am. Thanks."

"Now, we need to get a few things straight. For once, I need you not to babble and just listen to me."

"I don't babble" Sabrina grumbled.

"You do babble when you're nervous about telling me something" he smiled. "Now listen to me and listen good. I love you with all my heart Sabrina. You're my entire world and I'm not letting you go. EVER!! Knowing that you're carrying my child, that just......I don't know what to say about that except that it just humbles me. I'm not so sure that I deserve either of you but I'm sure as hell going to spend the rest of my life making sure you both know how much I love you.

Sabrina grabbed Alex and kissed him. "Oh Alex, I love you so much too. I was so afraid you wouldn't want this whole instant family thing I have going here" she laughed.

"How long have you known about the baby?"

"Just a few days ago. I just found out for sure last Friday. I have my first appointment with the OBGYN on Thursday if you want to come. You don't have to if you don't want to. I mean it's not like you'll be able to see or do anything. Besides, it's kind of last minute and I know that you're schedule is usually pretty tight..."

"Stop babbling Sabrina" Alex interrupted. "I'll be there. I wouldn't miss it for anything!"

WEDNESDAY TURNED OUT TO BE AN incredibly special day for Sabrina. She and Alex discussed getting married (she was now wearing the beautiful ring that Alex had given her) and they decided to let his parents know at dinner on Friday about all their news. Alex dropped Sabrina off at her office but getting any work done was extremely difficult. Alex kept calling to check on her about every hour. As endearing as that was, she had clients that needed her attention too. He picked her up after work and they spent that night making dinner together, snuggling on the couch and making love. Life indeed was getting better!

~

TRUE TO HIS WORD, ALEX WENT with Sabrina to her first doctor's appointment that Thursday. He was pacing back and forth in the small exam room waiting for the doctor to come in. Sabrina watched him with amusement as he made his third circle of the room.

Pushing his hand through his hair, for what must have been the fifth time; he looked over at Sabrina and saw that she was watching him. He walked over to where Sabrina was laying on the table and took her hand in his. "You okay baby?"

"I'm fine Alex, are you? You've been pacing nervously for a while now."

Alex started to respond but the door opened and the doctor walked in. He shook both his and Sabrina's hands and then spent some time talking about what she could expect, the vitamins he wanted her to continue taking, and eventually pulled in a machine so that they could hear the baby's heart beat.

After several minutes he found it and both Alex and Sabrina were in awe as they listened to the sound of his or her heart, proof that they had made a life together. Alex kissed the top of Sabrina's head and when she looked up; she saw that he had tears in his eyes.

As the doctor helped to pull Sabrina's top back down and gave her a hand to sit up, he sat on the stool and moved closer to her. "Now Sabrina, everything looks good but I've looked at the results from your hospital visit last Friday and we need to discuss what happened."

Sabrina felt Alex tense up but, thankfully, he kept quiet as the doctor continued speaking. "When you passed out last Friday it was due in large part, to your sugar levels. Knowing this is an issue early on in your pregnancy we need to keep a close eye on that. You're going to have to be extremely careful and watch that you're eating enough. Usually I'd let you go a month before you come back, but this puts you in the high risk category so I want you back here in two weeks. I know you've been nauseous and throwing up. If you continue to have trouble keeping anything down let me know so we can give you something to help. Get plenty of rest and if you continue getting lightheaded don't push yourself, just lay down until it passes." Smiling he touched her knee. "I know this is a lot but don't worry. This is my specialty and I'll take good care of you. Just listen to what I'm saying and you and your baby will be fine. Do you have any questions?"

Shaking her head Sabrina smiled back at him. "None that I can think of right now."

Shaking Alex's hand, the doctor told him to watch out for their girl and left the office. Sabrina was counting in her head, waiting for Alex's explosion. It took exactly five seconds before he turned towards her, anger simmering in his eyes.

"Hospital...passed out....trouble with your sugar. Jesus Christ Sabrina, when were you planning on telling me what happened? Why the hell didn't you call me right away! I should have been there! I had a right to know what was happening!"

"Alex I....."

"You what...didn't think I would want to know. Didn't think I'd want to be there. You what Sabrina?"

Shakily Sabrina scooted off the exam table and looked at Alex with tears in her eyes. "I'm sorry Alex. I didn't know what was wrong when it happened and I didn't want to reach out to you just because I was afraid. Kat and Sam were there when I passed out so they took me to the hospital. Honestly, I didn't even suspect I was pregnant until Kat put the symptoms together. Then when I found out I was, I didn't want to tell you until I knew how you felt about me. Not the baby or any guilt you may have felt, but about me!"

"Sam was there? And he didn't even bother to tell me? My own brother?"

"Don't you dare be mad at Sam! I begged him to not say anything to you. He didn't like it but he told me he'd give me a few days to handle it my way and if I didn't he was going to tell you himself. He had your back Alex; he was just being respectful in allowing me to be the one to tell you."

Grabbing her jacket and purse she went to the door, then turned back to Alex. "Four days Alex….I've just known about this four days longer than you. You're acting like I've kept this from you for months."

With that Sabrina walked out and slammed the door in Alex's stunned face. Hurrying through to the reception area she told the nurse sitting behind the desk that she would call in a few hours to schedule her next appointment, and quickly walked out to the elevator. After a few brief seconds of waiting and knowing that Alex would be catching up to her quickly she found the steps and started walking down, fuming the whole way about his reaction.

By the time she got to the bottom floor and exited the building, Alex was already on the street looking left and right for her. When he turned and saw her he hurried over to her and grabbed her elbow. "Where've you been" he asked worriedly.

"I took the stairs."

"The stairs" he asked incredulously. "You could have passed out again and I wouldn't have known where to find you. Of all the harebrained…"

Sabrina forcibly removed her arm from Alex's grip and started walking down the street.

Taking a deep breath to calm down, Alex walked up to catch Sabrina again. Stepping in front of her he grabbed her upper arms to stop her. "Look, I'm sorry. Can we have a seat on that bench over there to talk? Please?"

Hesitating a few seconds she finally acquiesced by nodding her head. Alex led her over and sat down beside her on the bench, their thighs touching. Taking her hand in his he apologized again.

"Truly Sabrina, I'm sorry for reacting that way. I got scared. Just thinking about what happened to you and I wasn't there bothers me. Plus, hearing the term high risk where my child is concerned is a little unnerving."

"For me too Alex, but you can't get mad. You've never gotten mad at me like that."

"I know. I've never felt so helpless before."

Sighing Sabrina rubbed Alex's hand. "We're okay Alex. The baby and I are fine."

"I know. Just takes some getting used to. I'll make you a deal. I'll calm down if you'll promise not to walk away when we have arguments."

"I wasn't walking away Alex; I was just putting some space between us to get some perspective. I promised you, no more running, and I meant that. You need to have a little more faith."

"Humpft"

Standing up Sabrina pulled on Alex's arm. "Come on baby. Your child and I are hungry. Feed us."

Smiling Alex allowed her to pull him to his feet and lead him to a restaurant down the street.

~

ALEX TOOK A HOLD OF SABRINA'S hand to help her out of the car. "Why are you so nervous? My parents love you."

"I'm about to tell them that I'm knocked up and, oh by the way, your son's marrying me. Doesn't exactly start marriage out on a good note does it?"

Chuckling Alex pulled Sabrina into his arms. "First of all, I'm marrying you because I love you more than life itself. The baby is a bonus that my parents will love and dote on and be extremely happy about. Stop worrying."

"And why are we here? I thought we were meeting them at a restaurant." Looking over she noticed another car in the driveway. "And why are Kat and Sam here?"

Rolling his eyes towards the sky, and praying for patience, Alex explained, "Mom decided she wanted to cook for her family because we all haven't been together in a while and Sam and Kat are here because, well, they're family. Is this a hormonal thing that's getting you all nerved up."

Sabrina elbowed him in the stomach and continued to walk up to the front door. Just as she got there the door swung open and Elizabeth Deluca pulled Sabrina into a hug.

"Oh Sabrina, I'm so happy to see you again." Looking over her shoulder she asked "What's wrong with Alex? He's doubled over."

Smiling pleasantly Sabrina released Elizabeth and made to walk past her. "He's just picking up something he dropped."

Elizabeth frowned at Alex. "Stop fooling around Alex and get in here."

Taking a few deep breaths Alex just smiled and walked up to the front door. Kissing his mom on the cheek he entered the house to see Sabrina wrapped in his father's arms in a big hug.

Releasing her he turned and hugged Alex then walked over by the kitchen door. "What can I get everybody to drink?"

Sam and Kat were sitting on the couch and stood up to hug the newcomers. Indicating they were set on drinks they sat back down. Alex asked for a glass of wine and Sabrina asked for juice. Raising his eyebrow, Joseph Deluca headed into the kitchen.

When Joseph came back in he handed them their drinks and sat on the arm of the chair that Elizabeth was occupying. "So what's new" she asked.

Alex and Sam and Kat looked at each other and started laughing while Sabrina frowned at them. Finally Alex stopped and walked over and put his arm across Sabrina's shoulder. "Actually, Mom, Dad, we have some good news to share with you both." Smiling into Sabrina's eyes he said, "Sabrina has finally agreed to marry me."

Both of his parents jumped up and went over to fold Sabrina and Alex into their arms. "Oh we're so happy for you both" his Mom exclaimed. "This is the best news ever!"

"Actually" Alex began, "It gets better than that."

Both of his parents turned towards Kat and Sam, looking expectantly. Sam just raised his hand laughing.

"Oh no....don't look at us. We're very happy just the way we are, right Kat?"

Sabrina looked to her friend and realized that the smile she plastered on her face didn't quite reach her eyes. "Absolutely" she confirmed to Sam.

"Well then" Elizabeth asked, "what's better than my son getting married?"

"Sabrina's pregnant. We're having a baby" Alex explained.

It took a few seconds before it really dawned on Alex's parents what he said. Then, as if the skies parted, they realized what he said and hugged them both again. "That's so exciting" Elizabeth cried. "I'm going to be a grandmother. I can't believe it!! Joseph, can you believe it. Grandparents, finally!"

~

AFTER DINNER EVERYBODY RETREATED TO THE living room to relax and have coffee and dessert. Alex and Sam separated themselves from the group and walked over to the fireplace.

"Okay, spill it Alex. You've been looking at me funny all evening. What's up?

"Nothing. I just wanted to say thanks."

"For what" Sam asked confused.

"For being there for Sabrina. She said you were there to take her to the hospital when she passed out. I wish it had been me there but if it wasn't me, I'm glad it was you taking care of her."

"I'm glad she told you man. I thought she should have called you right away, but she seemed desperate at the time and I just didn't want to upset her any more than she already was."

"You did the right thing Sam. I just wanted to tell you I appreciated that you had my back. She said you gave her a deadline before you told me yourself."

"Well" Sam began, "it all worked out for the best. I'm really happy for you Alex."

"Thanks Sam. By the way, when we decide on the date I was wondering if you would be my Best Man?"

Sam reached out to shake Alex's hand. "I'd be honored" he began then caught a few words that his Mom was saying. Nodding in their direction he laughed. "Looks like it may be sooner rather than later. Did you just hear what Mom was saying?"

Alex let go of his brother's hand and walked over to the couch where his mom was talking to Sabrina.

"….and you wouldn't want to worry about being too close to your due date" she was saying.

"Mom, what are you two talking about?" He glanced at Sabrina to see if she was upset.

"You're not pushing Sabrina into anything are you? We just got engaged and haven't even talked about when or where yet."

Sabrina smiled up at Alex. "It's okay Alex; she was mentioning that it probably wouldn't be a good idea to wait too long, and I think she's right. We should either get married soon or wait until after the baby is born."

"Absolutely not" Alex growled. "We're not waiting until after my kid is born. When he or she comes into this would it will be with my name and with his parents legally married."

"How about a June wedding" his Mom said.

"That's not a lot of time to plan mom" Alex said.

Sabrina looked over shoulder at Alex. "What's to plan? You me and a Justice of the Peace."

Frowning Elizabeth looked at Sabrina. "We can do a little better than that I think honey."

Alex walked around the couch, sat down beside Sabrina and took her hand. "Don't you want a big wedding baby? Don't girls spend their early years dreaming of their wedding day?"

Smiling sadly she said, "Alex, there's no reason to go through all that. My parents are gone, I really don't have anybody to invite. I'd want Kat to stand with me but other than that there's no one else to invite."

"Well that's just not true" Alex's mom began. "You have all of us and we'd be there for you just as much as we'd be there for Alex." Getting into the planning she continued, "We could do it at the beach house at the Cape in June. It would be simple yet elegant. We could construct an arch with your favorite flowers around right on the beach and have the ceremony at sunset. Then, we could all go back to the deck and have a catered dinner.

It could be really beautiful Sabrina. Between you and me and Kat we could pull everything together by June and make it truly special."

Joy lighting her eyes, Sabrina looked to Alex. "Actually that sounds lovely to me. Alex, what do you think?"

Bringing her hand up and kissing it he looked at her and smiled. "I think it's perfect. June it is then!"

Chapter 21

SABRINA SAT IN THE CHAIR NEXT to the window looking out at the ocean. From where she sat, she could see the arch she, Kat and Alex's mom had decorated just the day before. Elizabeth Deluca was a Godsend to Sabrina. She made planning the wedding so much fun and helped bring in small details that would serve as a remembrance of her parents during the ceremony.

When she first started discussing the wedding she had planned on just wearing something simple. Kat and Elizabeth immediately took control, and before she knew what happened, she found herself in a bridal shop trying on wedding gowns. The fourth gown she tried on convinced her that they were right, and that she should wear a beautiful gown to her wedding.

Just as the sun was setting, Joseph Deluca knocked on Sabrina's door for her walk down the aisle. Kat answered his knock, and then walked back in to the room to kiss Sabrina's check. Grabbing her bouquet she winked at her best friend and walked out the door to begin her journey down the aisle. Mr. Deluca walked over to Sabrina and took a hold of her hand. Smiling into her eyes, he leaned down and kissed her on the cheek.

"You look beautiful honey. My son is a lucky man."

Shyly Sabrina smiled up at him. "Thank you. I think I'm the one who got lucky though."

Taking her hand and placing it on his arm he moved her towards the door. "We better start heading out before Alex gets any more impatient. I swear he's been antsy all day today and it was starting to wear on my last nerve." Sabrina smiled and started walking forward when Joseph stopped her again. "Now honey, I only met your Dad briefly and I realize I didn't know him all that well, but I just know that he'd be so proud of you today. I'm no replacement for him but I want you to know that I'm proud of you too. I couldn't be happier that you're marrying my son and that I think of you as my daughter, and that no matter what happens from this moment on, I'm here for you too, not just Alex."

Sabrina reached up and swept Joseph into a big hug. She pulled back and, with tears in her eyes, she looked at Alex's father. "Thank you for saying that. I'm so lucky to have you in my life. I miss my Dad but, knowing I have you now, somehow makes it a little easier."

Joseph patted her hand and kissed cheek "Well, we better get this wedding started hadn't we?"

Wiping a tear from her eye, Sabrina nodded then grabbed her bouquet from the shelf on the way out to meet her future husband.

ALEX WAITED ANXIOUSLY AT THE ALTAR for his soon to be wife. Not that he thought she would change her mind, but knowing how commitment had been something she avoided like the plague almost her entire life, still worried him.

When the music started he looked up so see Kat as she made her way down the aisle. That's certainly a good sign he thought.

As Kat passed Alex to stand on the other side she winked at him putting him at ease. His head then turned toward the makeshift aisle and watched as his father led Sabrina out from the house.

She was stunning! There were no other words Alex could find except that she was absolutely stunning. Dressed in a strapless empire, ivory chiffon gown she began her descent from the back steps beside his dad. The fitted bodice lovingly hugged her breasts with a satin sash along her ribs. The long flowing pleated skirt of silk chiffon fell to the ground, barely hiding the gentle swell of her stomach that protected his child. Her gown lengthened in the back to form a longer train that trailed behind as she made her way towards him. She walked with graceful steps and when Alex looked down, he saw her pink tipped toes peak out from the bottom of her gown. She was barefoot!

When she finally approached him, his father stopped a few feet short, kissed her on the cheek and placed her hand in his. They both then turned to the minister and the ceremony began.

~

ALEX WATCHED AS HIS NEW WIFE laughed with their guests. Several tables had been set up on the back deck to accommodate the fifteen guests that his mother insisted had to attend. Not wanting to upset too many family members they only invited the ones that she felt were most important.

Although it was a small outdoor wedding, they still adhered to most of the normal practices of the toast, cutting the wedding cake, the bouquet toss but, most especially, the first dance for the bride and groom. Alex had never felt happier than when he was dancing the first dance with his beautiful bride. As the evening wore on he went over to where she was standing talking to his family and took hold of her hand.

"Excuse me but I'd like to steal my bride for a little walk on the beach." Smiling indulgently they motioned for him to take her away.

When they were almost at the water's edge Alex turned and took Sabrina in his arms. After a few brief seconds of looking in her eyes he leaned in and took possession of her mouth.

When he pulled away Sabrina smiled at him. "Wow! What was that about?"

"I missed you. There are far too many people around you tonight." Sabrina turned to look out over the water. With her back against Alex's chest and his arms wrapped tightly around her they were silent for a while, just enjoying the sound and smell of the ocean.

"What are you thinking baby" Alex asked.

"Just about how lucky I am. We've been through so much in the past year or so. I was thinking of how we met, what awful circumstances brought us together. We're blessed Alex. We need to spend every day together, living our life to the fullest. We need to honor the memory of those that didn't make it."

Sighing Alex pulled Sabrina even closer. "I know baby. You already are by what you're doing with *Loving Hands*. We'll find more ways too, I promise. I think of that day a lot myself, especially now that we've found our way, together. I wonder sometimes why us."

"Divine Intervention" she whispered.

Turning to face Alex she took his face in her hands and kissed him gently. "I think some kind of divine intervention brought us together. I'll forever be grateful for you Alex."

Bringing her head against his chest he cupped the back of her head and looked out to the ocean. "Me too baby" he whispered. "Me too."

Epilogue

ALEX AND SABRINA WERE WALKING ALONG the beach, hand in hand with their feet just touching the waves as they came ashore.

Hearing their daughter's laughter just up ahead, they looked up to see Elizabeth and Joseph pick her up and swing her as if they were going to toss her in the ocean.

"I'm not sure who's wearing out whom at this point" Sabrina laughed.

"Oh I think Hailey knows what she's doing. For a two year old she's pretty quick. She knows that if she wears her grandparents out she has a better chance of getting anything she wants. I know my daughter; she's hoping they'll be so tired they'll give in on anything just to make her happy."

Sabrina leaned into Alex's side. "Tired baby?"

Sabrina rubbed her hand over her stomach, trying to make the tiny foot that seemed to be sticking in her ribs move. "I think your son thinks he's playing soccer in here."

Alex reached over and placed his hand on her stomach. "Jeez, he's definitely moving around in there. Wanna go sit on the deck for a while and rest."

"I'm good but thanks. Moving seems to help."

Looking past where Alex's parents were playing with Hailey, they saw Kat and Sam turn around to walk back towards them.

"Ut oh" Alex smiled. "Looks like Sam is making Kat go back to the house. She doesn't look very happy right now."

Sabrina was smiling as Kat and Sam approached them. Seeing the frown on her friend's face she stopped and waited for Kat to reach her. Before she could say anything Kat started.

"Honest to God Brie, you better tell Sam to back off or your husband will have to go swimming to save his little brother's ass!"

"And just what do you want me to say to YOUR husband Kat? What's he doing now?"

Sam stood beside Kat with a frown on his face not saying anything.

"What's he doing? What's he doing you ask" she yelled, her voice going higher.

Sam rolled his eyes and murmured under his breath, "God save me from pregnant hormonal women."

Hearing what his brother said Alex busted out laughing. "Oh Dude, I can't believe you just said that."

Kat swung around to face Sam with her hands on her hips and tears in her eyes. "I can't believe you just said that Sam."

Sighing heavily he shook his head and took Kat in his arms. "I'm just worried about you honey. You're like twelve months pregnant and should be resting on the deck not walking on the beach!"

Kat pulled away and swatted at Sam's arm. "I just look tweve months pregnant Sam, I'm not actually that far gone!"

Chuckling he took her back in his arms and kissed the top of her head as he rubbed her belly. "I know but you're close to delivering and I'd rather be close enough to a car or phone to get you where you need to be. Can we go back to the house now" he asked forlornly?

"Yes. I am kind of hungry!" Leaning up she kissed Sam on the lips, smiled at Alex and Sabrina and headed to the house.

Sam watched Kat as she walked away and smiled as he turned back to the other couple. "She drives me daft but I love that woman!" Chuckling he ran to catch up to his wife.

Sabrina went back into Alex's arms and squeezed him tight. Turning her head she watched as another wave crashed on to the shore, then looked to where her daughter was playing with her grandparents. Rubbing her swollen belly she said, "we are truly blessed Alex. Truly blessed!"

P.L. Byers has loved romance novels since she was a young girl. After reading her first romance novel, *The Flame and the Flower* by Kathleen E. Woodiwiss, a romance novel was never far from her grasp. This deep love became a dream that someday she would be a writer too.

P.L. Byers lives in Franklin Massachusetts with her husband and son (when he's home from college) and two spoiled cats.

www.plbyers.com